The man glanced at her. The coat, open now from the strong wind that kept blowing, revealed just how thin the child was. For a moment the man hesitated, his conscience disturbed him slightly. He knew that what he was about to do was wrong, but he had had just enough whisky that night not to really care. It had been a long time since he'd had a young girl.

Holloway House Originals by Donald Goines

DOPEFIEND
WHORESON
BLACK GANGSTER
STREET PLAYERS
WHITE MAN'S JUSTICE,
   BLACK MAN'S GRIEF
BLACK GIRL LOST
CRIME PARTNERS
CRY REVENGE
DADDY COOL
DEATH LIST
ELDORADO RED
INNER CITY HOODLUM
KENYATTA'S ESCAPE
KENYATTA'S LAST HIT
NEVER DIE ALONE
SWAMP MAN

Special Preview of *Kenyatta's Escape*—page 185

BLACK
GIRL
LOST

Donald Goines

An Original Holloway House Edition
HOLLOWAY HOUSE PUBLISHING COMPANY
LOS ANGELES, CALIFORNIA

BLACK GIRL LOST

Published by
HOLLOWAY HOUSE PUBLISHING COMPANY
8060 Melrose Avenue, Los Angeles, CA 90046

International Standard Book Number 0-87067-988-0
Printed in the United States of America

Cover photo by Jeffrey. Posed by professional model.

DEDICATION

In the memory of a very good friend of mine, Archie Walker, who was killed at Detroit Metropolitan Airport on November 1, 1973...shot down in the parking lot by killers who didn't have the sense to get it for themselves. They had to try and take it from him.

1

THE SOUNDS COMING from inside the house were more than just loud and helter-skelter. "You black motherfucker!" The cuss word seemed to fill the night air whirling around the child who stood shivering in Los Angeles' early March wind. Suddenly the sound of a bottle breaking came to her. Next many voices raised at once, until another voice could be heard overriding the rest.

The loud confusion that the people inside called partying was an everyday occurrence at the house, as the child well knew. This was not the first time she had come here looking for her mother. More often than not, her mother could be found in the corn whisky house quicker than home.

As the early morning wind whipped around and through the young child, she clutched the summer coat she wore more tightly to her. All the buttons were missing, and in places she had pins holding the coat together. But as was the problem with buttons, she didn't own enough pins to do the job properly. Even though she was cold and shivering, and her teeth chattered, she still couldn't make up her mind whether or not to go in. She feared her mother's anger to such a degree that she had been standing outside for over an hour in the cold, waiting and hoping that her mother would come out by herself.

The house was a small frame building with the dingy gray paint peeling. It sat back from the street, and there was a small concrete pathway that led up to the door. But in most places the sidewalk was busted. On each side of the sidewalk leading up to the house were hedges, while in front of the house were bushes that stood as high or higher than a man standing straight up.

The streetlight in front of the house was out, so the only light that penetrated the darkness was the little bit that came out from the tightly drawn shades of the house. But the darkness was not what the small child feared. After all, at home on many occasions their house had been in complete darkness because of an unpaid electric bill.

Undecided, she stood there shivering. For the thousandth time, she almost found the courage to enter the house and ask for her mother. What drove her on was the hunger pains that kept flashing across her stomach. She bent over double as a cramp hit her in the stomach. Tears rolled down her cheeks as she remembered her mother's words early that morning, "Now don't go out, Sandra. It's too cold out today. I'll bring back something for breakfast in a little while."

At times, when her mother hadn't started drinking, Sandra felt an affection for her. But when her mother drank, which was the majority of the time, Sandra shied away from her mother in fear. She had received too many beatings from her mother when she had been drinking. Most of the times for nothing, for in her drunken condition she believed Sandra had disobeyed one of her orders earlier in the day.

"Hi there, littl' sis." The voice coming from out of the darkness made Sandra jump. "What you doing out in all this cold by yourself?" The man asked kindly, but Sandra noticed a slur in it.

From past experience, Sandra realized instantly that the man had been drinking. This would have surprised the man speaking to her, because he knew he carried his whisky well. Many grown women wouldn't have been able to recognize that he had taken a drink, let alone that he was loaded, so it didn't even cross his mind that the nine-year-old child in front of him was well aware that he had been drinking.

"I'm waiting for my mother," Sandra said slowly, as she began to hope that here was a chance to get her mother out of the corn whisky joint if she could get the man to go inside and get her out.

"Oh, gal, you're wasting your time. Your mother went over to Littl' Joe's place about two hours ago," he said, hoping the child didn't know any better. He didn't even know the child's mother. He had stopped down here on Hooper Street, since he was on the East Side, and decided to pick up a bottle of corn whisky. He didn't really like the stuff, but he had met a woman who had just come to the West Coast from the South, and the woman swore she loved corn whisky better than she did bonded whisky. She wasn't the first person he'd met like that, though. Many people out of the South preferred drinking good corn whisky to that which you could buy in the stores.

Sandra moaned and leaned over in pain. She couldn't stop the tears. She didn't even know where Littl' Joe's place was, nor did she have any reason to doubt the man's words.

"What you crying for?" he inquired softly as he glanced around, hoping that the child's mother didn't come out the front door.

"Momma was supposed to give me some money so that I could get something to eat," she answered honestly, hoping that the kind man would offer her a quarter or something near that sum.

"Come along, child," he said, taking her firmly by the arm and leading her down the walkway. "I'll drive you around to Littl' Joe's place. Then you can get your mother. How does that sound?"

It didn't sound too good at all to Sandra. Her mother would be furious at her for riding in a man's car, especially a man that she didn't know. She glanced up at the man. All men or women older than fifteen were elderly to her. She tried, but she couldn't remember when or where she had seen him before. Her mother had so many men friends that it was hard to remember them all. Even her mother was hard pushed to remember every last one of them. This one was tall, dark-complexioned, with a heavy mustache. His eyes, under deep, black brows, were pools of shimmering black ivory, now filled with a cunning lust.

As the young girl hesitated, he added, "If your mother's not there, I'll stop and buy you a hamburger or something, okay?"

As the cold wind blasted her thin coat open, she pulled her arm free to clutch the coat tightly. Hunger overcame reason and she somehow found the nerve to say, "I wish you would get me the hamburger first. I ain't ate since this morning." This was true.

The man glanced at her. The coat, open now from the strong wind that kept blowing, revealed just how thin the child was. For a moment the man hesitated, his conscience disturbed him slightly. He knew that what he was about to do was wrong, but he had had just enough whisky that night not to really care. It had been a long time since he'd had a young girl. He reached out and got another grip on her arm. He almost dragged her to the car. He opened the passenger side first and put her in, then almost ran around the car. He got in and started up the motor. The warmth from the heater quickly filled the car.

Sandra sat back and relaxed. After being out in the cold so long the heat felt good. She closed her eyes and enjoyed the warmth. The thin coat opened since she didn't have to clutch it around her and she put her hands in her lap. Her eyes closed, but she managed to fight off the sleep.

"You're a sonofabitch," the man said to himself as he observed the young kid next to him. With her coat open, he could see just how poor she was. Her legs were so thin that she seemed deformed. That coat with no buttons on it couldn't possibly keep the child warm, he reasoned. What kind of mother could the child have, he wondered, as he took his time and examined her. The mini-dress she wore was too small, besides being a spring dress. He reached over and felt the material. The dress was stiff from being out in the cold. He pulled her across the seat and put his arm around her.

She was so drowsy that she snuggled up against him. He put his arm around the child and held her protectively. As he touched her bare arm he could feel how cold she was. Her teeth had begun to chatter uncontrollably, but as he held her tightly, she relaxed.

He started the car up and pulled away from the curb. He removed his arm from around her and dropped it down on her leg, only to remove it with shame. Her leg was so small that he could almost put his hand around her thigh.

Basically he was a decent sort of man. He was

about to commit an act that he had never done before. He was also in the habit of talking to himself whenever he was alone. Now, with the child dozing beside him, he had time to think about what he was about to do. He decided to stop and get her something to eat first. She never woke up as he parked in front of an all-night restaurant. He left the motor running so that she would be warm, ran into the restaurant and ordered her a chicken dinner with mashed potatoes and navy beans. Then he ordered her a slice of apple pie, with a small container of milk

He pulled away from the restaurant and drove until he found a dark side street. He parked on it and woke her up. "Here Sandra," he said as he shook her awake. He waited until she wiped the sleep out of her eyes and then put the dinner in her lap.

She blinked as she came awake. She could feel the hot dinner on her lap, but she couldn't believe it. For a brief moment, Sandra thought that she was dreaming. She glanced up at the strange man, then back at the dinner on her lap. She opened it up slowly, and as she stared at the food her stomach growled loudly and tears ran down her cheek. Saliva ran out of the side of her mouth as she reached for the first piece of meat.

The man, watching her out of the corner of his eye, began to really feel self-conscious as he realized that the child was really hungry. He wondered idly how long it had been since the kid had had a good meal. Had he asked, Sandra could have told him that it had been over five days since she'd had any kind of food similar to the dinner in her lap. She'd had hot dogs to eat, and her mother had made her a jelly sandwich for dinner two days past, but nothing like what she held in her lap. Her stomach growled again as she lit into the food. She didn't waste time with a fork or spoon. She picked up a handful of mashed potatoes and crammed them down her throat. She ate like an animal.

The man had to look away, not in disgust but in pity. As he watched the child he realized he could never go through with what he had planned. There was no way now for him to take advantage of the child. He felt too much pity for her. She seemed to have caught too much hell already in life for him to come along and force himself on her.

As he uncorked his whisky bottle and took a long swig, he thought, "How the hell could I ever have even thought about doing something to this child?" He cursed at himself, and then the idea of some man attempting to take advantage of one of his daughters flashed across his mind. He had three of them but they were all damn near grown now. He pictured them as they were when they were Sandra's age. The thought of a man attempting to do to one of them what he had started to do with Sandra filled him with rage. Then shame overcame him and he couldn't think of enough things to do for the child. At first he toyed with the idea of taking her home, but in a minute he rejected that idea. It would never work, and besides, he'd be getting in trouble with the police if the child's mother complained about her missing. Next, he wished that he could meet Sandra's mother. He'd tell the sorry bitch a few things!

As she finished with the dinner and licked her fingers, he removed the pie from the bag and gave it to her. She looked up at him with wonderment. Her big eyes seemed to swim with gratitude as she tried to smile at him.

"How old are you, child?" he asked as he took another swig from the half empty bottle.

"Eight," She replied around a mouth full of pie. She ate the pie quickly, as if she was afraid someone would take it away from her. He gave her the milk and watched as she gulped it down.

The man took another swig from the bottle, then dropped his hand down on her leg. He slowly ran it up her small thigh, feeling the heat that had now replaced the cold. He put his arm around her again and pulled her closer, as she tried to clean up the mess she had made while eating.

They sat in the car quietly, Sandra enjoying the heat, while the man allowed himself the small pleasure of rubbing the young girl's leg. His hand moved higher under the thin dress. She opened her eyes and glanced up at him. She had no fear of him since he had been so kind to her. It was so seldom that she came in contact with kindness that she didn't believe he would hurt her. From past experience, she knew that the man was feeling on her. Many times in the past—ever since she could remember—one of her mother's friends had put his hands on her in this fashion. Always after they drank too much, one of the men would try and feel her whenever her mother wasn't paying attention. She had never been hurt by it, so in her child's mind she didn't have any reason to fear it. Nor did she dislike it, because attention was something she very seldom got. She could recall times when she had gone out of her way to sit on the lap of a man who she knew liked to rub on her. When he finished he'd slip her a dime or nickel, depending on what kind of change he had in his pocket.

Again this man in the car found himself in the clutches of the strong drink. His hand began to ramble higher and higher under the child's dress. He fought with his desires, but since she wasn't putting up any resistance he continued to roam.

As Sandra felt his hand pushing the small panties aside, panic gripped her. Fear of the unknown overcame her, and she blurted out, "Please, Mister. Please, don't hurt me!"

Her words had a sobering effect on him and he snatched his hand from under her dress. As she stared up at him, he looked away, too ashamed to look at her.

"I'll take you home," he murmured, so low that she hardly heard him. As he started up the motor, shame was a growing thing inside of him. Years later in life, whenever he remembered this night, shame would overcome him. He realized as he drove through the silent streets of L. A. that he had almost committed a crime that would have filled him with so much guilt and shame that he seriously doubted if he'd have been able to live with himself.

2

THE CHILLING WINTER mornings were just about gone as Sandra stood on the corner of 48th Street and Hoover, but she still had one problem—her daily search for food. She was constantly hungry, because seldom did she get enough to really fill her up. As she stopped in front of Sammy's liquor store, the hunger pains almost caused her to double up.

Suddenly there was a knock on the window and the sharp noise brought her out of her daydream of food. A table full of all kinds of food was what she always dreamed about. She glanced up and saw Sammy, the owner of the store, smiling kindly at her from inside. He motioned for the young girl to enter and Sandra noticed as she came through that the store was empty.

She grinned up at Sammy and he smiled in return. "You want to sweep up today?" he asked in that funny way of his.

Without replying she ran into the back of the store and got the broom out. She knew where everything was kept. When she came back to the front of the store Sammy was busy waiting on a customer. She began sweeping and it didn't take long before she was finished with the light work he had asked her to do.

When she came back from putting the broom up, Sammy asked, "How come you no go to school today?" His smile was broad on his wrinkled face, and his snow white hair was still thick and bushy.

Sandra just shrugged her shoulders. She didn't want to tell the kind old man that she had been too hungry when she got up to think of school. After looking in the refrigerator and finding it empty as always, she had known that she couldn't sit in a classroom all day. Not without lunch money.

She didn't have to answer Sammy, though. He could tell from what she selected as pay for sweeping up what her problem was. He had known that the child was hungry as she stood outside the store. He had seen the look on too many faces when he was in a concentration camp in Germany. The look of hunger was the same no matter where you were at. He felt sorry for the child, but there was nothing he could really do but help her out like he did whenever she came by. She was really too young for him to hire, so he gave her food whenever she came by. It wasn't necessary for her to sweep up for him, but she seemed to want to feel that she was earning her way. He watched her pick up a pack of cheap lunch meat, then some crackers.

"Here," Sammy said as he walked over and got her a pop out of the box. Next he picked up a cake and gave that to her, too.

Sandra's eyes were shining as she left the store, clutching the food tightly to her thin chest. She almost ran all the way home. Sammy watched her leave, with pity in his kind eyes. It was a shame, he knew. He knew the child's mother, a drunk who didn't care about anything but where her next drink was coming from. She had been in his store early that morning, buying her daily bottle of whisky. He gritted his teeth and went back behind the counter.

When Sandra arrived home, she hesitated briefly. She didn't want to run into her mother now. She listened outside the door for a minute, making sure there were no sounds from inside, then turned the knob and went in. The house was deserted just as she'd hoped it would be. She carried her tightly clutched bundle into the kitchen and sat down. There was no bread so she made small sandwiches with the crackers. She opened her pop. It was a treat, what with the cake and all. Sometimes when Sammy was busy with customers she'd go in and steal a can of sardines or something else small. Then her conscience would bother her. Because Sammy was so good to her, she really hated to take anything from him without his knowing it.

The sound of a key being put in the door caused her to jam the rest of the tiny sandwiches into her mouth. By the time her mother staggered into the kitchen she had eaten up everything but the cake.

Her mother, a thin, brown-complexioned woman, swayed on her feet, then rocked back in her high heeled shoes. Her eyes were bloodshot, while the dress she wore was dirty. One of her stockings was rolled down halfway on her leg, while the other one was put on right. At one time her mother could have been called slightly attractive. She had a small nose and her hair was a dark brown. But from the constant use of alcohol, her looks were deteriorating.

And now a silence filled the small room—a waiting silence that stifled the air, heightened the glare of the ceiling light, moved the walls inward, sealing them in. "Well now, Miss Lady, why ain't you in school?" her mother asked with sarcasm.

For a minute Sandra started to lie, then decided on the truth. "I was hungry. When I got up there wasn't nothing to eat, so since I didn't have lunch money, I didn't go."

Just for a minute her mother was quiet, taken aback by the answer. Then she put her hands on her hips. "You kids nowadays are full of shit," she yelled loudly. "When I was your age we went hungry at times, but we took our asses to school. You didn't have lunch money! What the fuck do you think I am, a money tree? Hell, you ain't no little spoiled white kid! Lunch money my ass." She reached down and snatched up the cake. "You had enough money to buy this shit with. I know you, you little bitch. You been going through my pocketbook taking my change, that's what you've been doing." She started to eat the cake as she rocked back on her heels.

"I ain't took nothin' from you!" Sandra screamed as she jumped up and made a grab for the cake. "Give me back my cake!" She yelled loudly as her mother continued to cram the cake down her throat.

"I'll give you hell and call it cake," her mother retorted as she pushed the screaming child away. As her mother made a motion towards the bottle of pop, Sandra leaped in front of her and snatched the pop out of her reach. She ran around the table, attempting to drain the bottle dry.

"You better not drink all that pop, you little bitch," her mother ordered sharply. Sandra continued to drain the bottle until it was empty, ignoring the order. She managed to keep the table between them as her mother continued trying to reach her.

A loud knock on the door interrupted the fight before it could get worse. A loud man's voice could be heard. "Sandie, open the goddamn door," a man ordered.

Though both women had the same name, most people called Sandra's mother Sandie instead of Sandra. As she staggered towards the door, she made Sandra a promise. "I ain't forgetting, littl' whor'," she swore over her shoulder.

Sandra wasn't worried about the threat. She knew her mother would either forget or be in a completely different mood by the time they met again. She watched as her mother opened the door and led the man in. He was carrying a bottle of whisky. Sandie didn't even stop in the living room. They continued straight on to the bedroom. Then her mother came back out and got two glasses, ignoring her daughter completely, as if she was just another piece of the kitchen furniture.

Sandra sat in the kitchen, not really knowing what to do. Now that she was full, she silently wished that she was in school. But then she remembered the way the kids talked about her clothes and decided that she didn't want to be in school. If she never went back to school she'd be happy. The school children had started to call her Raggedy Ann, a nickname she would have rather done without.

The sounds of the bedsprings brought her back to reality. She knew then that she'd have to leave the house. She couldn't stand to hear the sounds her mother made when she was drunk and in her bedroom. Sandra quickly got up and left the tiny apartment, slamming the door behind her. She walked from Broadway down to 51st Street, all the way to Western, and then back. She stopped in a small store that was crowded and stole a small cherry pie. She went back out and down the street eating the pie.

Later in the day she went into a supermarket and stole two packs of cold lunch meat. She took this so that she'd have something to eat when she got up in the morning. She ate one package of the meat and saved the other one. What she wanted most, though, were some clothes, but she didn't know how to steal them. She knew that that would be the only way she'd ever get some. If she had some nice skirts she'd be able to go to school without the kids getting down on her. The more she thought about it, the more she wanted the clothes.

She remembered that there was a shopping center up on Slauson Avenue, so she slowly started walking in that direction. It didn't disturb her that it was over twenty blocks away. The thought of catching a bus was out of the question. It was something only the rich did, so she believed. At ten years of age, she couldn't remember ever being on a bus. Her mother never had any reason to take her anywhere.

She noticed older girls putting their thumbs out and getting rides, but that possibility didn't cross her mind. She believed she was too young and nobody would pick her up. Even though she was tall for her age her chest was as flat as a boy's, and with the clothes she wore she didn't appear too attractive. She would have had trouble trying to get a ride. She looked too much like a boy.

An hour later she reached the department store parking lot. She went in the back door of the large store. When she reached the children's department it was crowded. She picked up an empty bag and walked around until she found the skirts and blouses. She didn't know what size she wore so she held the skirts up in front of her. When she found what she thought would fit she selected four of them and put them in her shopping bag. Two black women shopping noticed the child stealing and laughed, but it frightened Sandra so that she only managed to stuff two blouses into the bag. She almost dropped the bag and ran, but she wanted the clothes too bad. The saleswomen in the department had noticed the child. Sandra walked back out the way she had come in, swinging her bag happily. Now she could go to school without any trouble. If she had enough money for lunch every day she wouldn't have any problem, she reasoned, as she made her way out of the store.

3

BY THE TIME SANDRA reached the age of thirteen she had solved her lunch money problem. She knew how to steal now. She had been caught five times in the past three years, but it didn't disturb her once she knew what would happen. Most of the time they'd turn her loose in the store after talking to her. Only one time had they taken her down to juvenile, and since they'd had so much trouble trying to reach her mother, the policewomen had just given up and sent her home. It wouldn't have made any difference whether or not they'd given her car fare because she now knew how to stick her finger out and get a ride. With the short skirts she wore no man would mistake

her for a boy, even though she wore her hair in a short
natural.

When a stranger met Sandra. he or she was not
overwhelmed by any sign of intellectual maturity, but
on the other hand, she was a product of circumstances,
which had been hard and were still hard. She still
skipped school whenever she felt like it, not because
of lunch money or hunger. Now it was because she
wanted the time to go downtown and hustle the stores.
Inside of her there was a driving desire to accumulate
a large bankroll. She had a morbid fear of being completely broke. She hoarded money as if it might disappear. She would never allow herself to spend her
last dollar. She always kept at least two or three dollars hidden under her mattress at home. It was abnor-
mal for a child of that age to be so concerned with
money, but if she hadn't taken an interest in her own
money affairs, she would have starved to death,
because her mother just didn't care. Or if she cared,
she didn't stay sober long enough to follow up her
good intentions.

Sandra jumped out of the car on Western and waved
merrily at the young brother who had given her the
lift all the way from Hollywood and Vine to 38th
Street and Western. She clutched the bag to her. Inside
was the short leather coat a young prostitute had been
worrying her to get. The price tag was sixty-five dollars, so she figured on making at least thirty dollars
off the white coat.

As she attempted to cross the street, a Cadillac

came tearing around the corner. As she jumped back out of the way, the rider on the passenger side tossed a package out the window. As she watched the package roll under a parked car, she almost got run over by a police car that came roaring around the corner behind the Cadillac.

Dope! The word exploded in her head as she rushed over and reached under the car for the package. Some of the onlookers watched her curiously as she straightened back up, but she didn't care. She had what she wanted, even though she didn't really know what was in the small brown package. She rushed down the street, wanting to get away before the men in the Cadillac came back and tried to redeem their package. The little white skirt she wore flapped up high against her butt as she took long steps, putting as much distance between her and that corner as she could. She stopped on 41st Street and delivered the leather coat.

"Honey, I ain't got but twenty-five dollars in the house," the young blonde prostitute stated, slowly fingering the soft leather.

If it hadn't been for the package that was burning her pocket, Sandra would never have left the jacket, but now all she wanted to do was get home and see what she had "Okay, I'll let it go for that this time, but don't do that no more. If you state a price, I look for you to pay it if I get the piece you want," Sandra warned the girl coldly.

As Sandra let herself out of the woman's apartment,

she overheard the girl say to her pimp, who had been watching the transaction, "That's goin' to be one cold-hearted bitch when she gets older."

"She'd be a bad bitch for somebody if she wasn't so damn young," the pimp replied loudly. "Give her a couple more years, then I might shoot at her myself."

When Sandra reached the street, she took the back way. She hurried down to Van Ness and started walking. A young brother drove past slowly, his car broke down in the back, showing that he was a low rider. He gave her the eye and she stuck out her hand.

He quickly slammed on his brakes and waited for her. She ran out to the car and jumped in. As soon as he got a close look at her, he cursed. "Shit! I thought you were older, baby. You ain't hardly over twelve, are you?"

"I'm sixteen," she lied quickly. "But if you don't want to give me the lift, that's up to you." She didn't make any attempt to get out, though.

He grinned. "Sixteen my ass. If you're a day over fourteen, I'll give you some cap."

She didn't understand what he meant, but she replied, "Look man, if you want, I'll pay you for the ride. How about that?"

"You got some cash, honey?" he asked quickly. Then he pulled into a gas station. "How much gas should I get?" he asked and grinned.

Sandra removed a five dollar bill. "How about two dollars worth?" she inquired. She wasn't frightened of him. She was used to dealing with young men. He didn't seem to be over eighteen. She stared at him with her large eyes. She had the same eyes her mother had. Large bedroom eyes. He looked away.

"Sure baby, two dollars will be fine." He started to say something else but the arrival of the gas station attendant interrupted him.

"Would you stop and let me pick up the Temptations' latest album at the record shop?" she asked lightly, not really caring if he stopped or not.

He hesitated briefly, then introduced himself. "Most of my friends call me Fast Eddie, honey. What do they call you?"

"Sandra," she replied, not bothering to offer any other information.

"Well, Sandie," he began, but she interrupted sharply. "It ain't no Sandie, mister. It's Sandra." Her voice was sharp.

Eddie glanced at her quickly. "Damn, baby. I do believe you are sixteen. Ain't no kid goin' to speak to no man in that tone of voice. In fact," he added, "when I use that tone, I'm either speaking to my dog or to someone I don't like."

"I'm sorry," she stated, then continued, "I just don't like for anyone to call me Sandie. That's my mother's name, and I don't want to use her name no way. No kind of way, if you know what I mean."

"All right," Eddie said easily. "It don't make me no kind of difference one way or the other. What I'm interested in is what you goin' to give me for taking you to the record shop, then takin' you home."

"How about if you just keep the change from the five dollar bill. Would that be all right?"

Eddie shrugged his wide shoulders. "That's cool with me," he stated, as he mentally counted the money he had in his pocket. He realized quickly that he'd still be three dollars short on his fix money. Well, he reasoned, three dollars was easier to hustle up than the whole ten dollars that he needed every day.

After Sandra picked up her record, Eddie dropped her off at the dilapidated tenant building that she stayed in. He glanced at the building and commented, "Your landlord must have something against paint, huh?"

She hadn't understood what he meant, and as she turned and stared up at him he just shrugged his shoulders as he realized that she hadn't understood. "That's okay, baby," he said lightly. "If it doesn't bother you, it sure ain't no sweat off my nuts."

Again she didn't understand him. At school the teachers thought she was a truculent child in some instances, and in others they just believed she was a half-wit. But in both cases they were wrong. What Sandra did in school was all for a reason. Ever since she had been sent to school in clothes that made the other kids laugh, she had started to pretend that she was retarded so that she wouldn't be called on and made to stand in front of the whole class. What she had started continued to follow her as she went through school. The teachers expected it from her, so they didn't disturb her. Some of them even believed she couldn't read, while many of her classmates knew that she skipped school sometimes so that she could go sit in the public library and read all day.

What the teachers didn't realize was the fact that she had been so ashamed of the other kids' comments that she had developed a protective schizophrenia to meet the problem. When called on by a teacher to stand up and speak, she spoke in a low voice and ran her words together so that no one could really understand what she was saying. It became so exasperating that the teacher would stop calling on her.

But now as she sat in the car in front of her house listening to Eddie and not understanding what he meant, she wondered if she was really dumb. She was not pretending illiteracy now. She just couldn't understand what he meant. "Okay, baby," he said as she opened the car door, "I'll be seeing you around."

As soon as she got out, he pulled off, not realizing that he had left a mixed up child behind. But what she couldn't understand was his cold remark about the building she stayed in. She didn't have any standards to go by. Every place she had ever lived in had been run down. She didn't understand anything about a ghetto, because she had never lived in anything but a ghetto. Her world was small, and being an only child she had no one to talk to. She lived in her books, the ones she stole from the library. They were her real world.

When Sandra reached her apartment, she could hear the noise coming from inside. Her mother was entertaining again. For a second, she wasn't going to go in, but then she remembered the package she had picked up. She opened the door and entered. Couples danced together closely, as the record player blasted out the latest hit.

Sandie spotted her daughter as soon as she entered. Noticing the album she carried, Sandie rushed over. "What's that you're carrying?" she asked loudly.

Sandra passed over the new album and continued on into her bedroom. She didn't feel like arguing with her mother today. In a minute the sound of the new album filled the apartment. Sandra sat on the bed and opened the package. A number of small balloons rolled out. Each one contained something. Now she knew it was dope. She counted the balloons. There were twenty of them. She didn't even bother to open one. She had seen the boys at school open one up and snort the white stuff that was inside the balloon. She carried the package to her closet and hid it way in the back, where she knew her mother would never find it. Then she quickly forgot about it. There was too much noise coming from the group of adults, so she changed clothes quickly and left. Her mother didn't bother to inquire as to where she was going, because she didn't really care.

Sandie knew that her daughter was stealing, even though Sandra had never told her that she was. But from the clothes she brought home, the mother knew. But as long as her daughter continued to bring her a dress home now and then it didn't make any difference. If she ended up in reform school, it was her own problem, not Sandie's. That was the way her mother looked at it.

After Sandra left the house, she walked around aimlessly, until she found herself in front of Sammy's store. He grinned at her as she came in and bought a pop and cake.

"Hey Sandra," he said on the spur of the moment, "how'd you like a job in the store in the evenings after school?" He was surprised at his own question. One moment he was thinking that she was growing up, looking nice in her neat little skirt, and the next moment he was offering her a job.

"Sure, Sammy," she replied quickly. "I'd like that fine." Frequently things happen in life that will change the future of a person. This was to be a big step in Sandra's life—one she would always remember.

In the following weeks Sandra would show up at the store with her school books in her arms. Sammy's wife would sometimes be in the store, and on those days she would take Sandra in the back of the store and both of them would study Sandra's English book. Sammy's wife was from the old country and wanted to learn to speak English, so Sandra helped her. But in helping, she helped herself.

In a matter of a month there was an astonishing change that took place in Sandra. Even her teachers couldn't believe it. In fact, they didn't want to believe that what they had been so sure was a half-witted child was actually one with an agile mind. One reason for

the abrupt change was that Sandra didn't have anything to be ashamed of any more. Her clothes were
as good or better now than most of the girls in the
class. So she wasn't ashamed to stand up in front of
the class and recite. Only now, instead of saying, *if'n*,
eatin', or *show 'im*, she spoke perfect English. Clear,
bright and articulate was Sandra's speech. But it
shouldn't have surprised anyone, because she was a
voracious reader. Actually, the only ones surprised
were her schoolteachers, because her schoolmates had
known all along that Sandra was anything but dumb.

One Friday when Sandra showed up for work,
Sammy came quickly from behind the counter.
"Come, I want to show you something," he said and
led her from the store, leaving his wife in charge. He
took her to the nearest bank and showed her how to
open an account. Since it was payday for her, he put
five dollars in her account. When Sandra left the bank,
her eyes were bright. She had found a new experience
in life, something that would always keep the fear of
hunger at bay. As long as she had money in the bank,
she'd never have to worry, she reasoned.

As they left the bank, Sammy glanced down at her
and grinned. He knew her mother was starting to take
most of her paycheck, so he'd decided to show her
how to put her money where her own mother couldn't
reach it. He didn't realize just how much of a problem he had solved for Sandra.

4

THE SUMMER WENT BY smoothly for Sandra. She had stopped stealing because there was no reason for it now. She had all the money she needed, and her clothes were more than adequate for her needs. With an abundance of food she had started to fill out, all except her breasts, which were going to be small anyway. She ate constantly, always nibbling on something until Sammy had commented, "One day, Sandra, if you continue to eat like that, you're going to weigh over three hundred pounds!"

She laughed and continued to eat. Eddie had stopped in the store one day for some wine and found her there alone. Sammy was in the back of the store.

"Well, well, if it ain't youngblood. What's happenin' sweet thing? I know you ain't forgot me."

"No, I ain't forgot you," she replied softly.

"Good, good," he replied, then walked out of the store without paying her for the bottle of wine or cigarettes she had given him across the counter.

Sandra didn't say anything. She walked over and got her purse and counted the money out for the wine and cigarettes. Sammy had watched the whole thing from the lookout slot in the back of the store. He watched as she counted out the change from her purse and put it in the register. He smiled softly, and impatiently he brushed back a tear that appeared in the corner of his eye. He loved honesty. It was a quality in a person that always won him over.

He came out from the back of the store. "You know, Sandra, I been thinking. You've worked for us quite a while now. Maybe it's time we gave you a little raise. Maybe ten dollars more a week, okay?"

Sandra glanced up into his kind face. She was so glad that he hadn't seen what had just happened. She didn't know how she could have explained Eddie taking the stuff out without paying for it. Sammy was so kind that at times, when she thought about how it would have been to have a father, she wished that he would have been like Sammy. While working in the store she was never aware of a racial problem, until one of her mother's drunk friends came in and called Sammy a name. When she blushed in shame Sammy looked at her and laughed it off. What they said didn't disturb him, he said, because a drunk rarely knew what he was saying anyway. But she was mad the rest of the day.

Only when Eddie came in the store was Sammy different. He watched Eddie closely. Sometimes Eddie would pick her up after work. "What's with that honkie?" Eddie would ask. "He acts like he's your father or something."

"Don't call him no honkie," she'd reply hotly. "I mean it, Eddie. He's got a name, and it sure ain't honkie."

"Okay, okay, baby. You still goin' to loan me the eight dollars?" he inquired. He'd blown his loan one night by referring to Sammy as a peckerwood. Sandra had got hot and jumped out of the car. Now he knew that if he wanted his blow money it was best not to talk about the old white dude. Sandra was a strange young girl. At times she didn't act like a young girl. He knew she liked his company, but when he tried to get close to her she froze up. He could kiss her, but that was as far as it went. He was beginning to believe she was really a virgin.

"What you wantin' with the money, Eddie? I mean, I really want to know what you're doing with it. You don't drink that much wine, so it must be stuff, huh?" she asked sharply.

Eddie glanced up quickly. At first he was furious with her for asking, then he decided that he didn't give a damn anyway. He only got about ten dollars a week out of her, so he didn't have that much to lose.

"Yeah, baby, I want to buy me a fix," he stated harshly, not caring one way or the other what she thought about it.

On the other hand, Sandra didn't care either. She had wanted to save the eight dollars he'd asked for, so that she could put it in the bank on Monday. She gave a sigh of relief. "Well, if that's all you want, I got a balloon at home I found. You can have that, and I'll save my eight dollars."

"Shit!" Eddie exclaimed loudly. "You probably ain't found nothing but some damn bunk. I want some dope, girl. I don't want no bullshit."

"It ain't bunk. It's dope," she replied coldly. "If it was junk I'd have thrown it away long ago."

"How you know what it is? You don't use," Eddie continued the argument.

"Well, if you don't want it, it's up to you," she answered coldly, "but I bet it's more in the balloon I'm goin' give you than in the one you was goin' to buy."

Eddie didn't answer, he just turned and started driving in the direction of her home. When they reached her apartment building he asked, "Can I come up and fix there? I got my outfit with me."

Sandra hesitated briefly. "Well, I guess it would be all right if my mother ain't home." She wasn't worried about her mother catching Eddie fixing. She was worried about the hell she knew her mother would raise when she found Eddie in the apartment. Sandra had never taken a boy to their place, so she knew her mother would have something to say. Since it was payday, she didn't have to worry though. A few dollars would smooth over her mother's hurt feelings.

Eddie got out of the car and followed her into the old apartment building. The stairs they went up were run down and needed repair. He stood back as she stopped in front of the apartment and listened. Then she opened the door. The inside wasn't any different than any of the other crummy apartments he had been inside.

"Have a seat," Sandra said after they entered, and she went on into a bedroom. In a second she was back, carrying a red balloon in her hand.

Eddie's eyes got big as he saw the size of the balloon. "It must be at least a spoon," he said to himself as he stared at the object in her hand.

She tossed it to him. He caught it and felt how full it was. With his teeth he bit it open and the dope fell out. Sandra gave him a piece of newspaper to hold under the bag. The stuff tasted bitter and dark. Then he slowly removed his outfit from his pocket.

"You better take it in the bathroom in case my mother comes in," Sandra cautioned.

"Yeah, yeah, I know what you mean," he said, not really knowing, too concerned with the dope in his hand.

Sandra followed him into the toilet. She stood back, leaning against the wall, and watched him shake out a small amount from the balloon into his cooker. He removed matches from his pocket and struck three of

them and held them under his cooker. The dope inside
the empty wine top dissolved quickly. He set the cooker down on top of the toilet seat and removed his belt.
He twisted it around his arm, slowly squeezing his fist
until he found a vein that suited his need.

Sandra watched closely. It was the first time she
had ever seen anyone really cook up some dope,
though she had heard about it often enough. She
watched, fascinated, as he drew up the drug into the
needle, then stuck it into his arm. He got a hit quickly. Blood rushed back into the bulb and he slowly
removed the tie from around his arm, then shot the
dope. Before he could take the needle out of his arm,
his eyes closed and his head dropped down on his
chest.

Instantly Sandra became frightened. "Eddie, Eddie,
you got to wake up," she yelled. When that didn't do
any good she reached over and pinched his arm until
he lifted his head. His eyes rolled back in his head
until she could only see the whites of them.

"Oh, my God," she moaned, then started to slap his
face, the way she did the drunks when she had to
awaken them so that they could go home early in the
morning. Slowly his eyes regained some sort of focus.
She didn't stop working on his face until he opened
his eyes and spoke. "Goddamn, that sure in the hell
ain't no bunk. Shit! It must be raw dope. That shit
can be cut. Baby, you don't know what you got there,
do you?" He stared at her foolishly, trying to get his
mind right.

"Yeah, I know what I got now," Sandra said sharply, her eyes never leaving his face. The possibilities of what she had didn't escape her whatsoever.

"You got some more of this?" he inquired, showing that he truly was himself again.

"No, all I had was that balloon I gave you. You want to give me a little of that back?" Sandra asked quickly.

"That wouldn't be right," Eddie replied. "You said I could have the balloon and I didn't shoot it all because I was trying to save some. Now you want me to give that back to you." He didn't bother to add that, if he had shot it all, he'd more than likely have been dead. Eddie knew the dope was raw uncut dope. The bag he had would bring him close to two hundred dollars once he cut it and sold it himself. He decided his best bet was to get away from Sandra as fast as he could. That way she wouldn't bother about asking for any of the stuff back.

Sandra had to hold back a smile as she watched Eddie prepare to leave. He rolled up the rest of the dope, making sure the balloon was folded inside some newspaper so that whatever drug fell out would still be wrapped up inside the newspaper. He almost ran out of the apartment since he was in such a hurry to find out how much of a cut the dope would stand.

Sandra knew from his actions she had something good. She took a hot bath and went to bed, waiting patiently for the next day when she'd be in school. She knew just how to get rid of the dope. She had thought about it for the past few months, but had never put her plan into action because she hadn't known just what she had. Now that she knew, she didn't waste any time.

The next day in school she searched the corridors until she found the boy she had been looking for. Chink was a young boy who looked so much like a monkey that the rest of the kids had started calling him Chink. She had started speaking to the bashful young boy months ago. Chink wasn't in any of her classes, but she knew him and knew about him. He was the school's pusher. He was a short, dark-complexioned boy, with long muscular arms. He was strong and was known to be a mean fighter, but when it came to girls he was scared to death of them. He couldn't look one in the eye. He'd dance from one foot to the other whenever one talked to him, which was rare because the girls acted like they were afraid of him.

When Sandra approached him in the hall she had a hard time keeping him cornered while she talked to him. "I want to see you after school, man. You hear me, Chink. I want you to wait for me outside the front door."

Chink heard her all right, but he couldn't stand still. He wasn't really frightened. He just didn't know how to act around girls. Since he lived with just his father behind the poolroom his father ran, he never was near any women. He liked Sandra, she was one of the few girls, if not the only one in the whole school who spoke to him every time she saw him, and it didn't seem to make any difference to her who she was with. If she was with other girls (even though it made Chink nervous when she was) she would still go out of her way to speak to him. Now she wanted him to wait for her outside of school. He knew that he'd do it, but he hated the idea of it. Standing out there where everyone could see him waiting for a girl.

"I'll be lookin' for you, man," she said, leaving him in the hall. He sighed with relief as she departed, but he was still wondering what she wanted. It couldn't be dope, he told himself, because he knew everybody who used in the school, and she didn't hang out with none of that crowd. His mind was in a turmoil the rest of the day, wondering what was the reason. It didn't bother his schoolwork though, because he was another one of the practicing illiterate children that fill the ghetto schools. Chink suffered from the same problems that Sandra had. When he was younger, he had a clothes problem, but his main problem was his face. He hated the ridicule so much that he tried to become invisible. He couldn't stand for a teacher to call on him in a classroom. So he pretended to be mentally disturbed. With his looks, it wasn't hard to fool the teachers. Most of the young white schoolteachers couldn't stand to look upon his features without shivering anyway, and he knew this. He could sense it. As soon as one of them turned away from him, shaking, he knew what the reason was. He couldn't change himself to please them, so he tried to make himself invisible.

The day passed slowly for Sandra. She constantly watched the clock on the wall of her homeroom. At ten minutes to three, she gathered her books together. She didn't want anything to slow her down. At two minutes to three she got up and moved to an empty desk near the door. When the bell rang, she was the first one out of the homeroom. She raced toward the front door. She had just about reached it when she saw Chink coming from the opposite direction. She stopped and waited for him.

Chink was in such a hurry that he didn't notice her in the bunch of children rushing for the door. He went out the door and then stopped and stood around, not knowing what to do. He felt like everyone was watching him. He would have bolted and run, but his curiosity and his humble respect for Sandra wouldn't allow him to take such a cowardly way out.

He saw her as soon as she came out the door and glanced the other way. "Hey, big man," she said lightly as she came up, "what you trying to do, ignore me?" She was only joking with him, but her words started him to shifting from one foot to the other.

Chink glanced at her, then looked away. He couldn't stand to look her in the eyes. "What's wrong, boy?" she said, still joking with him."'Cause you got on them sharp ass threads, you think you big shit, huh." Now she had him. Chink dressed above average. His clothes cost more than any of the other kids could afford. He dressed sharp every day, but he didn't want to be reminded of it. Her direct attack embarrassed him and he blushed down to his shoes.

His constant movement gave Sandra a feeling of being a complete woman. She knew he was embarrassed by being near her. It was a new experience for her. The total power of a woman over a man. She enjoyed the feeling. When some friends passed and yelled out at them, she enjoyed his embarrassment. She took his arm and wrapped hers around it. "You goin' walk me to work," she stated. She felt his muscular arm tighten up under her fingers, but he followed her on down the street. He kept his head down and shuffled along beside her. When one of the addicts came up and spoke to him, he didn't know how to handle it with Sandra beside him.

She handled it for him. "Go on, man, and take care of your business. I'll be waiting right here." She stopped and leaned against a rotting fence.

Chink walked off a few feet, removed a small balloon, and gave it to the young drug addict. Sandra watched as money was exchanged between them. When Chink returned, she gave him a big smile, revealing beautiful white, evenly spaced teeth.

"Don't worry, man. That's what I wanted to talk to you about," she said lightly.

Chink stopped in his tracks. He wasn't going to start her off on drugs no matter how much she begged. He really liked and respected Sandra. He remembered when she used to come to school as raggedy as he was, and he knew that her mother hadn't bought the nice clothes she wore. He respected her for being able to go out into the streets and get what she wanted, but he wasn't about to make a drug addict out of her.

"If it's drugs you want, gal, I ain't about to sell you none," he stated point-blank. For the first time he glanced up and looked her directly in the eyes. "I mean it, Sandra."

"Well, I'll be damn," Sandra replied, surprised. "But it ain't no drugs that I want to buy. I want you to sell some drugs for me," she stated as she took his arm and started him on down the street.

Now it was Chink's turn to be surprised. He stared at her with his mouth open, unable to speak.

"Boy, if you don't close your mouth," she said lightly, "you goin' end up catchin' you a mouthful of flies." She laughed, then removed the balloon from her bra and gave it to him. "I don't know how many times you can cut it. All I know is it can be cut, Chink. I done already had an addict test it and he almost fell out 'cause it was too strong."

They walked along in silence with Chink carrying the dope. He finally asked, "Where did the dope come from?"

By the time they reached the store where Sandra worked she had explained everything to Chink, even to how much dope she had hidden. For some reason, she believed she could be honest with him. She took him on as a partner. They shook hands outside the store, then Chink went on his way to find out just how much cut the dope could stand.

The next morning before going to school, Sandra

dressed carefully in an expensive pants outfit she had stolen over the weekend. It was a form-fitting outfit, black, with a white blouse and black silk jacket. The price tag had been one hundred and twenty dollars. When she had inquired about it, the salesgirl had almost laughed in her face, knowing that the skinny black girl in front of her couldn't afford the expensive outfit. She had made a big joke out of it, displaying it as if she knew she had a sale, until Sandra had made up her mind to steal the outfit, just to teach the girl a lesson. Sandra knew she couldn't go back into the store again, since the girl had more than likely missed the outfit as soon as Sandra had left. Sandra glanced in her cracked mirror at herself, and she liked what she saw. She quickly gathered up her books and left the apartment, not knowing if her mother had come in or not.

As soon as she came out of the apartment building she found Chink waiting on her. "Hi, honey," she said sweetly, causing him to drop his head and blush. She examined him while his head was down. He was wearing a pair of gray pants with a matching leather jacket. The clothes, being expensive, covered his muscular body to perfection.

He took her books from her. "That stuff was sure 'nuff smokin', Sandra. It knocked them junkies to their knees," he said and held out a roll of money.

She slowly counted the roll of money. "It's over two hundred dollars here," she said surprised. "You ain't took your share out yet, have you?"

"Aw naw, Sandra, I can wait till next time before I takes out mine," he said, speaking flatly, with his head down.

Sandra counted the money again, then split it in half. "Here, I told you yesterday that we was goin' cut the money in half," she said as she pushed his share into his hand. Then as he took the money she reached over and lifted up his chin. "Listen, Chink, when you talk to me, don't give me that shufflin' shit you use in school. And quit speaking like you just come from Georgia or Mississippi, boy. You ain't country, so stop actin' like it. Be a man. I don't like boys," she stated coldly.

As they continued on toward school, he lifted his head up and took pride in the fact that he was walking next to the best dressed girl in school. He noticed the large mannish looking hat she wore. It made her look like a boy, but the black outfit she wore was all female. Every line of her slim body was shown to its best advantage, and he gloried in the fact that he was walking beside this young fine brown frame. When they passed other kids and the kids yelled out at them, he found himself walking in a more cattish manner.

Sandra noticed the change in him but remained silent. For some reason, she found herself drawn to the husky boy next to her. There was nothing handsome about him, but he wasn't as ugly as the silly girls in school liked to pretend he was. His long arms were loaded with muscle, and when she looked in his eyes, she found them to be bright and alert, with a smoldering intelligence that he couldn't hide.

From that day on they walked to school and came home together. Some days she'd lead him over to the library. At first he had rebelled, until she picked out certain books and made him promise her that he'd take them home and read them. And once she started him reading, he was addicted. He sometimes took her arm and led her over to the library where he'd wait patiently until she picked out some books for him. The summer passed swiftly for them until all of her dope was gone, and in its place she had a bank account that was over three thousand dollars. She made Chink start an account and together they put up some money and Chink bought some dope and continued to sell it for the both of them.

One evening after she got paid, she left the store. As soon as she started to walk up the street she noticed a car pull up beside her. "Hey, baby, how about a ride?" She glanced over and saw Eddie.

"No, honey, that's all right. I'm expectin' somebody to pick me up," she said, speaking the truth. Chink had just bought an old car and she had been looking for him out the window of the store. She figured he must have got held up and decided to walk on home.

"Come on, honey," Eddie said, his voice shaking slightly. For the first time she really took notice of him. His nose was running and his eyes were watery. She knew at once that he was sick, but it didn't bring any pity out of her. Over the months she had count-

ed up how much money she had given to him and it
was over a hundred dollars, so she had decided that
that must come to a stop. He was nothing to her, so
it wasn't her problem trying to help him keep up his
habit.

He parked the car and came around the front of it.
"Here girl, what's with this funny shit? You act like
I done did something to you!" he exclaimed loudly.

"It ain't that, Eddie. It's just that I ain't got no
money to give you, and I know that's all you want.
You don't never stop by until Friday when I get paid,
so I don't need you, man," she stated coldly, looking
him in the eye.

For a minute he was surprised, then anger took
over. He had depended on her to get his fix money,
and now the silly young bitch was coming down on
him. He grabbed at her, only to find a switchblade
knife descending on his arm, and he just barely
snatched his arm back in time. Now he was really
mad. "Fool ass young bitch," he snarled angrily. "You
damn near cut me," he said.

"If you put your hands on me, I am going to cut
you," she answered him honestly.

Before the words were out of her mouth his hand
flashed out and he slapped her viciously across the
face. His hand was a blur as he slapped her again.
Then when she attempted to bring up the knife, he
knocked it from her hand. He stepped in close and
slapped her viciously, until her head rocked on her
shoulders. She tried to scratch him, but he was too

swift for her.

Tears of anger flowed down her cheeks as she tried to fight him back. When he demanded the money she cursed him harshly. He slapped her again. Suddenly he was gone, and she fought back the tears so that she could see.

Chink had him by the back of his neck, then spun him around and smashed a huge fist into Eddie's face, again and again. The fight was as lopsided as her effort had been against Eddie. Eddie didn't stand a chance.

Sandra had never seen Chink angry and now she hoped she never would again. He moved with the swiftness of a hunting cat, his strength was that of a bull, and his anger was that of a man that has found himself loving something and then seeing someone trying to destroy it.

Chink couldn't have explained to himself the rage that overcame him when he drove up and saw Eddie slapping Sandra around. This slim girl was the only thing he cared for in the whole fuckin' world, and he had known in that minute he'd die before he'd allow anyone to harm her. He had burst from his car like a mad bull, goaded beyond any thought but to kill that which offended him.

As Eddie slumped to his feet, Sandra grabbed one of Chink's arms and tried to drag him away from the bloody bundle that lay at his feet, but Chink's arm was like a band of steel. Her small strength was nothing, and he didn't even feel her pulling on him. It took four men who had come up to watch the fight to get him off of Eddie, and they had a job of holding the young boy back from killing the older one on the ground.

"Chink, Chink!" she screamed and threw herself into his arms, fixing her small body against his so that he couldn't help but notice who it was. Sandra was as tall as Chink, but that was where the comparison ended. For a brief minute he almost tossed her away from him, but she clung to him. Her arms were locked around his muscular neck and as he rocked his wide body back and forth, she was swung almost off her feet. But she held tightly. He was like an enraged grizzly bear, but somehow she managed to get him back to his car.

"We got to leave, baby," she said over and over again. "The police will be here in a minute, and we don't need that." She pushed him into the car and ran around and jumped in the other side and started the motor. He had been giving her driving lessons in the evenings, so she could handle a car quite well.

Sandra drove over to her house and took him upstairs with her. She led him into her bedroom as if he was a child. And as they sat down on the edge of the bed, his huge frame shook from the passion that he had just been filled with. Sandra leaned over and kissed him tenderly. His arms encircled her until she believed she was held in a vise. He kissed her slowly, tenderly at first, then she returned his kisses until they found themselves making love. It was the first time for her and she cried out, but he was so tender that she stretched to meet his every move, until they were as one.

They made love the rest of the evening and through the early morning, until Sandra heard her mother come in drunk. She didn't bother to get up and neither did he. She lay in his arms until the sharp light from her door opening caused them both to roll out of the bed.

"Whore! No good bitch," her mother screamed at her drunkenly from the doorway. She yelled for her boyfriend to come in. "Kick that punk out of here," she ordered as her companion came into the bedroom behind her.

By this time Sandra had quickly dressed. "He ain't throwing nobody out," Sandra stated quietly. "I paid the fuckin' rent on this place for the past three months now, so ain't nobody that I like goin' get tossed out."

"Bitch, you ain't but fifteen years old. You don't order nobody around in here. I says who's goin' come in and who's not," her mother replied. She stepped forward to slap Sandra, but found herself staring at the switchblade knife her daughter held. "Ain't goin' be no slaps either," Sandra stated harshly, "'cause if you put your drunken hands on me, I'll cut your god-damn throat!"

Her mother stared at her speechless. She didn't know what to say, but she wasn't drunk enough to run up against the knife her daughter held. "I'm goin' call the police and have this nigger here put in jail for rape," she finally managed to say. "I'll fix his littl'

red wagon first, then I'll have your ass put in juvenile until you get some sense."

"And if you do," Sandra stated coldly, "there won't
be nobody to pay your rent for you." Her words
stopped her mother in her tracks. She had become too
accustomed to having her daughter pay the rent.

Chink removed a large bankroll from his pocket
and tossed eighty dollars on the bed. "There's this
month's or next month's rent. I'll stop by and pay your
rent each month, but Sandra is moving out of this flat.
If you want the money it's yours. If you want to go
to the police, it's up to you, but you won't get a penny
if you do."

Greed flashed across the mother's face. Her eyes
went to the money on the bed, then back to the young
couple. "Well now," she said, changing her tone,
"Sandra's old enough to do what she wants, but these
white folks don't think so. If ya get into any trouble
I'm just goin' say I don't know nothing about it, that's
all. Don't come begging me to stick my neck out if
something happens, and I expect you to bring me that
rent money on the first of every month, 'cause I needs
it." She picked up the money, then added, "This is
just enough for me to catch up on my back rent, so
I'll be expectin' some more on the first." She glanced
at her daughter, then dropped her eyes, because both
of them knew it was a lie.

Sandra didn't have any suitcases so she put her
clothes in brown shopping bags. Chink helped her
carry everything to the car. He was so happy he

couldn't believe it was really happening. Sandra was just as surprised. It had all happened so sudden. At three o'clock in the morning she found herself moving out on her own. But for some reason, with Chink beside her, she wasn't frightened of the move. It seemed as if it was all to the better.

They checked into a motel for the rest of the morning, and the next day Chink went out and found a dopefiend couple who rented an apartment for them. Chink paid three months in advance on a modern apartment on the west side of Los Angeles. Since they had the car they didn't have any problem getting back and forth to school. Since he was sixteen, Chink wanted to quit school, but Sandra raised so much hell about it he decided to stay on and their days in high school passed quickly. As time wore on each became more dependent on the other. For Chink, Sandra was his world. Everything he did was for her. And she felt the same way. She went out of her way to cook good dinners for him. Once she found out what he liked she'd spend hours in the kitchen getting it right for him. He had stopped her from stealing from the stores, and now he bought all her clothes. He still sold dope every day and his income was fairly large for a young couple. He bought a later model car, which was the beginning of the end. It drew attention to the young couple when they went to school. Now the teachers even whispered about them as they passed in the hallways together. They were too well dressed, and when they went to the lunch room, they bought whatever they wanted without concerning themselves about the cost. The other kids talked, and soon everybody in the school knew that they lived together.

Spring had just begun. They had passed the winter together with no problems and now that Sandra was sixteen they didn't think they had anything to worry about.

Chink stopped Sandra on the way to the lunch room. "I got to run home for a minute, baby, and pick up some more stuff. You want to ride with me or go ahead and eat?" he asked her during their lunch break.

"Naw, honey, I'm starving. I think I'll go ahead and eat. I'll see you when you get back," she answered quietly, then smiled at him. She couldn't have realized that it would be quite a while before they would meet again.

Chink had only a half hour so he left in a hurry. On the way back from the apartment he had a flat tire, so he left the car and caught a cab. As soon as the cab pulled up and he got out, detectives seemed to come out of the ground. He tried to swallow the dope but he had too many balloons on him. The school kids sitting by the windows saw it all. Chink went down under a flood of white and black detectives as they tried to reach him before he could swallow the stuff. He fought back, striking out with his huge arms. He broke a white detective's nose and blood gushed out as he screamed in pain. Another officer took his place and went down just as quickly. "Pin his arms," someone yelled, as the men scrambled around trying to hold tight to the struggling boy. One detective pulled his gun. "Step away from the black bastard," he roared loudly, pointing his gun at the struggling group.

By this time the fighting group of men was surrounded by kids that had run out of classrooms to see the fight. "Don't shoot him, you no good bastards," one of the braver kids yelled. "You got ten men. Ain't that enough to take one little black boy?"

And indeed it was enough. Now the detectives put their billy clubs to work, and Chink went down to stay, with his head bloody. The men rolled him over on his back and handcuffed him roughly. "That's one black bastard that's a bull," one of the white detectives said, giving a compliment but still stepping on the toes of the black officers who were beside him.

"What about the girl?" one of the detectives asked.

"She's probably still in school," a black officer answered. "We can walk in and pick her up now," he said and started off, followed by three white detectives.

When the school bell rang Sandra left her class, not aware of what had happened outside the school. When she passed two white men in the long hallway she took them to be schoolteachers. If she had bothered to glance behind her, she would have seen the men turn and start to follow her. She stopped at her locker and put her books up. Before she could close it, a black hand reached over and held it open.

"What's the idea, man?" she asked, without bothering to glance up to see who it was.

"We want to see what you have in your locker," the man answered.

This time she did glance up. Her senses reeled and spelled out police as she noticed the well-dressed black man leaning over her shoulder. Her glance quickly took in the white man next to him, then she turned and saw the other one.

"Damn, man," she exclaimed, fighting for time. She didn't have anything in her locker, but she hesitated anyway, trying to figure out what was happening.

Her slight hesitation made the officers think she had something to hide. One of them shoved her roughly out of the way. She struck her back on the handle and cursed loudly, "You white bastard," she swore.

They tossed everything out of her locker and went through it until they knew there was nothing in there to conceal. "Well, what now?" one of them asked.

"Well, we know she's in it up to her neck with him, so take her down too," another one ordered. And as they led her out of the school the teachers stood around helplessly and watched. Not one asked what the problem was. The rough handling of the girl meant nothing to them, as long as they weren't involved. The black teachers who watched shook in their shoes because they knew what the white police thought of all of them. They could and would be handled the same way if they so much as opened their mouths. As the police passed they each gave them a wide smile as if they had just arrested some notorious criminal instead of a sixteen-year-old girl.

They led Sandra out to the police car, and when she saw Chink in the backseat handcuffed and bleeding, her heart turned to stone.

One of the officers spoke to her. "Isn't this your boyfriend?" he asked harshly, trying to make his voice as cold as possible so that he would frighten her.

But instead of frightening her, it only made her grit her teeth in anger. The sight of Chink had been enough. Now the detective's voice on top of it filled her with unreasoning anger.

If his voice had been harsh, hers was chilling when she deemed to answer. "If you mean, honkie, do I give him some pussy every now and then, that's our business. Ain't got nothing to do with no peckerwood!"

The young white detective was shocked and his face showed it. One of the other white officers stepped up, thinking that he had to protect their image in front of the school kids who stood around. He couldn't allow no black kid to talk to them in that manner in front of such a large group of people. One of the black detectives had to fight back a smile. He had known it was coming. He could tell from the shock in her eyes when she saw her boyfriend in the car. He realized she was angry and would say just about whatever came into her mind and damn the consequences.

"You're a smart black bitch, ain't you?" the older officer said as he stepped up and slapped her. The only mistake he made was slapping her instead of using his fist, because the slap didn't even turn her head. She brought her knee up so fast he didn't even realize it was coming until pain exploded in his nuts and he folded up like a used bag, crying out in pain.

Now all the hours Chink had spent teaching her how to protect herself came into use. She moved coldly, as if she was standing outside herself. She didn't think she could win, but she could hurt this one white bastard in front of her. She moved so fast she took the officers by surprise. Knocking his hat from his head she grabbed a handful of hair and pulled his head toward her knee. She caught him in the middle of the face with a brutal, powerful blow that splattered blood over both of them. His head shot back as if his neck had broken, and before they could reach her she kicked him in the face again, breaking his nose.

They moved on her then, coming from all sides. Chink, watching from the backseat of the police car, cried out in his helplessness.

To the white officers who rushed at her, she was not a young black girl anymore—a schoolgirl at that. She was just someone black who had found the nerve to strike back at them. They couldn't tolerate it, and they rushed her with billy clubs, striking each other in their hurry to strike her. She went under them, holding her head for protection, until one well placed blow put her to sleep. Then she didn't feel the other blows that rained down on her prone body.

Chink, in his blind rage, with his hands cuffed behind his back, tried to butt his way out of the car, until one of the uniformed cops in the car caught him behind the ear with his club. As Chink sank down on the floor of the car, the cop spoke to his partner. "I know how the poor bastard must feel. If it was my old lady out there I'd want to kill the whole fuckin' bunch of them."

"Okay, okay, she's out!" one of the black detectives yelled and pushed white detectives out of the way. The murmurings from the crowd of schoolkids brought them back to their senses and to avoid a riot they controlled themselves.

As the detectives tossed her unconscious body into the car beside Chink, one of the white detectives muttered, "They ain't no better than a couple of damn animals, the way they act."

"No better," one of his friends commented. "That's all the fuck they are is animals."

The black officer who had been responsible for the arrest glanced at the two white officers who were speaking. He noticed the thirty-nine-dollar washable suits both men wore, then glanced into the car at Chink, who wore fifty-dollar pants and a pair of alligator shoes that must have cost a hundred dollars. For the first time he was ashamed that he was responsible for the arrest of the young couple. He knew just about everything there was to know about them. He wondered idly if the white cops who called them animals could have come from such hardships as children and survived as well as this young couple had. No, he doubted seriously if either one would have been able to pull himself up out of the ghetto as they had been trying to do.

5

SANDRA WALKED AROUND the apartment aimlessly. The past few weeks had been a nightmare come true, but now it was over. She had finally been released on probation for striking an officer, while Chink had been sent to juvenile until he became eighteen. Well, it wasn't too bad, she told herself for the thousandth time. It could have been worse. They had tried to pin something on her, but it had been impossible because she had never made a sale nor ever handled any of the dope. So eventually they had had to let her go. That she worked every day went in her favor, but from the small taste of law she had seen, she didn't want any more of it. For a black person to become involved with the law was trouble, spelled with large letters. It didn't make any difference if you were guilty or not. If you were black that was good enough to find you guilty.

Well, she decided, she wasn't in any bad shape. She had over a thousand dollars in cash money, plus there was over a thousand dollars worth of dope stashed around the apartment. The dope, she decided, would have to be left alone until she could figure out some way of moving it. It wouldn't be that much of a problem, though. If she could get in touch with the right drug addict, then the problem would solve itself. But common sense told her to take her time and use some kind of caution. It would work out better in the long run.

Suddenly there was a knock on the door, taking Sandra out of her daydreams. She peeped out the window before opening the door.

"Hi George, Betty," Sandra spoke politely as the couple came into the apartment. As she closed the door behind them she wondered idly what could they possibly want. Ever since the day Chink had used them to purchase the apartment for them, she hadn't seen them, except for one other occasion when they had come by and tried to buy some dope from Chink. She remembered his anger. He had gone into a rage because they had come to his home on such an errand. If there was one thing he didn't do, that was sell dope from his home, and the only reason they knew where he really stayed was because he had had to use them to get the apartment.

"Have a seat," Sandra offered as she waved her hand in the general direction of the couch.

George was a tall dark-complexioned addict with a scar on the side of his face, while his woman, Betty, was just the opposite of him. She was light-complexioned, with a blonde wig. Where he was tall, she was short and stocky. Her mouth was large, while her eyes had a dazed look about them, as if she was tripping out on LSD or something.

"We was wonderin'," George began, "uh, since Chink got busted, if we could cop from you." He raised his hand before she could interrupt. "I remember what Chink said about coming over here trying to cop, but since he is busted, I kind of thought that you might be handling the stuff yourself, maybe." He stared at her closely, his eyes never leaving Sandra's face.

"Well, first of all," Sandra replied, "I ain't dealing no stuff." She hesitated slightly, then added, "But there is a few drugs left. I was thinkin' about gettin' in touch with you to see if you wanted to handle it for me. It ain't that much, really, and after you get rid of it, there won't be any more, 'cause I don't have Chink's connect." She stopped suddenly, then corrected herself. "I mean, George, if by chance you would want to handle the littl' bit of stuff I got and help me get rid of it." She shrugged her shoulders and was so involved with what she was saying that she didn't notice the gleam that came into George's eyes at the mention of his handling some drugs.

"How much stuff do you have?" he asked, not able to conceal the greed in his voice.

A warning bell went off in Sandra's head. She studied him closely, then asked quickly, "Well, how much stuff did you come to buy?" She had a sudden inspiration and added, "You just might be purchasing all the stuff I got." She couldn't help but notice the way his shoulders dropped at her words, as if she had knocked out his main daydream.

"Oh," he said dejectedly, "we didn't want but a twenty-five-dollar spoon." He hesitated, then continued. "I know that won't wipe out your supply. At least, I hope it don't."

"No, I don't think that will wipe out my supply," Sandra replied, putting him at ease. "Ya excuse me for a minute," she added, then walked off to the bedroom. She removed the dope from the toe of one of her shoes and counted out the balloons. It was a good thing that Chink had already mixed and measured out everything, she reasoned, as she counted out nine twenty-five-dollar balloons. For a moment she wondered if she was doing the right thing. George and his woman were the only addicts that she really knew, so it didn't leave her too much of a choice. Oh well, she reasoned as she walked back into the living room, she didn't have that much to lose. If they didn't return with the money, the loss of the dope wasn't that much, as far as she was concerned. She still had twenty-two more balloons left and the sooner she got rid of them, the better off she'd feel.

"Here George," she said, handing him the dope. "There's eight twenty-five-dollar balloons there, plus the one you just bought." Sandra waited until George had counted out the bags of dope she had dropped in his hand. "It's two hundred dollars worth of stuff there, George, but all I want for it is one hundred and twenty-five dollars. You'll make seventy-five dollars out of it," she added.

"Shit!" he exclaimed loudly, "it ain't really enough dope here for me to start dealing! By the time people get the wire that I've got some stuff, I'll be out of it." He lifted his eyes up and stared at her closely. "You mean to tell me that this is all the dope you got?" he asked harshly.

For a brief second Sandra was startled by the tone of voice he used, then she pulled herself together. "It ain't none of your business how much stuff I got, George, but if you don't think I've given you enough to handle, just give it back. Ain't nobody twisting your arm making you sell it. I told you from the start that I didn't have that much, now if you want to down it for me, cool, if you don't, that's cool too." Her voice hadn't risen, but there was a firmness in it that couldn't be ignored.

From the way George tightened his fist with the dope in it, there was no doubt that he wanted the dope and had no intentions of giving it back. As Sandra examined him, she began to really doubt her actions. She knew at once that she had made a mistake giving the drugs to George; she tried to straighten it out. "When I went up and saw Chink last weekend, he suggested that I offer you the chance of getting rid of the few bags that I got. He wants me to bring the money up and put it in his account so you do what you want. I'm only carrying out his order."

At the mention of Chink's name, George's face changed. There was little doubt about it, the man was afraid of Chink. "How much time did you say Chink was doing?" he asked suddenly.

"I didn't say," she replied quietly, "but if you want to really know, I'll gladly tell you. He's got to stay in jail until he turns eighteen. His birthday is in February, so I believe he'll go to the parole board some time this year. More than likely, six months from now." She knew she lied, but from the facial expression George made, she deemed it well worthwhile. If George had any intention of putting shit on her for the money, he'd have second thoughts about the matter now.

"But to put your mind at ease, George, whenever you get rid of that dope I gave you, I still have enough to give you another bag."

As the words Sandra spoke penetrated his scheming mind, George smiled. As long as he knew there would be some more dope waiting whenever he got rid of this small amount that she had given him, he could get his game together. He didn't have any intention of ever bringing her all her money; all he had to do was figure out a way to get the rest of the stuff from her. "Since it ain't but a small amount of dope, Sandra, I don't see why you don't just give it all to me now. That way, I won't have to be rushing over here trying to catch up with you when I run out. If I had all the dope, you wouldn't have to worry about the police coming in on you and finding something, either."

For the first time since entering the apartment, Betty spoke up. "Yes indeed, Sandra. The best thing you could do would be to give all that shit to George. That way you won't have no worry. I'll bring you the money over as soon as George gets rid of the jive."

In the silence that followed you could hear the wind blowing outside. The tree branches could be heard as strong winds rocked them back and forth against the building. Sandra watched the scheming couple closely. She felt like she was being enclosed with two snakes. "I would if I could, George, but you wouldn't want me to go against Chink's order, would you?"

Every time she mentioned Chink's name, there was a noticeable change in George. This time sweat broke out on his forehead. He glanced at his woman, then asked, "Well Sandra, since we'll be only doing business with you, Chink wouldn't even have to know, now would he?" He winked at her, as if they were plotting something together.

"Oh yes," Sandra answered quickly. "I don't never do nothing against what Chink has said. Right now, I'm wondering if I should tell him about this conversation when I go up to see him this weekend."

There was no way for him to hide his fear now. His knees started to shake uncontrollably. "Don't do that, honey. I mean, I just mentioned it, that's all. We'll do it just like Chink wants. Yeah, just the way he wants it done. I was just offering my opinion, that's all."

Twenty minutes later Sandra was rid of them. She sighed with relief after they left. It had been a mistake to give them as much dope as she had, but it was too late to worry about it now, she reasoned. After taking a hot shower Sandra went to bed and sleep came slowly. She tossed and turned most of the night until the early morning traffic could be heard. Then, she suddenly fell asleep. She slept soundly until a loud knock awakened her. She sat up and rubbed her eyes. She didn't have the slightest idea of who it could be. After all, no one really knew she stayed there. She slipped a light green wrapper around her transparent nightgown and went to the door. She glanced out the window first, and the sight of George standing there only angered her.

She snatched the door open and demanded sharply, "What the…." That was as far as she got. Two other men pushed into the apartment. They had been concealed by staying close to the wall. The only way she could have seen them would have been to open the door and stick her head completely out of it.

The taller of the pair waved a gun at her. "Just shut your mouth, sister, and you ain't got to worry about gettin' hurt."

Sandra backed up until she felt the coffee table strike her in the back of the leg. Then she stopped and stared at the gunmen. The tall one was dark-complexioned with a nervous twitch in his left eye. She kept staring at it, and it seemed to jump every minute. The other man, who only had a knife, was short and stocky, brown-skinned and with a heavy black mustache. The men didn't pay any attention to George after pushing him into the apartment. Their complete attention was directed at her.

The tall gunman advanced on her "We don't want to give you no trouble, littl' sis, so just tell us where the dope and money is, and you won't get hurt."

"There ain't no money. We spent all the cash we had on lawyers," she managed to say, before the pistol came down and struck her a vicious blow in the face. Pain exploded on the side of her head like she had never felt before. Then she could feel hands lifting her back up to her feet. For a moment she wondered why had she fallen so easily. A male voice came through the fog that was trying to envelope her.

"Now littl' sis, we know you got the stuff somewhere in this joint, so just set it out."

The voice brought her back to reality. They wanted the little bit of money she had put up. She opened her eyes and saw the tall man leering down in her face. "Where is it, girl? Don't try and be hard, just set it out," he said, then slapped her across the face.

She raised her hand and pointed at George. "I gave him the dope last night, and he ain't brought no money back yet."

Both of the stick-up men laughed.

"Yeah, that sure was some good dope you gave to old George there, but honey, don't you go expectin' nothin' back from that shit. You know George is a dopefiend, so he ain't goin' know how to handle no dope without shootin' it all up." The shorter man said this in a heavy voice, then added, "Now if you was to give me and old Tree here a bag," he said, pointing at his partner, "you might just get some kind of money back for your trouble."

Sandra knew the man was lying, but if she refused to give up the dope there was no telling how far the men would go. She raised her hand and was surprised to feel blood running down the side of her face. "Even if I gave you the rest of the dope, you wouldn't bring back enough money to pay my rent here, let alone enough for us to try and cop some more stuff with," she replied, fighting for time, trying to think of a way out.

The two men smiled at each other. "Don't you worry about it, littl' sis, just give up the dope," the one called Tree said.

For a minute she hesitated. If she didn't do what they asked, she reasoned, they would use force. "Okay, okay," she said. "Look in the closet, down in a red pair of shoes, in the toe. It's all that's left," she added.

Tree had already rushed off. He came back out of the bedroom grinning, carrying the dope. "Now," he said as he approached her, "all you got to do is tell us where the money is. Then we'll leave you all alone."

It seemed as if her world was falling down around her. She had tried, but it hadn't worked, yet there was one thing she was determined to do, and that was hold onto the money at all costs. "There ain't no money," she stated. "If there had been, do you think I'd have taken a chance on giving him some dope?" She pointed at George, then added, "I must have needed money badly to take a chance like that." She noticed the men hesitate and glance at each other undecidedly. They had no way of knowing if she had any money or not, she reasoned.

Tree moved suddenly. He stepped up and ripped her gown down around her waist. She opened her eyes and saw that she was half naked. "Damn, girl, you ain't got no tits, but you is kind of young. If you don't want to be gorged, you better come on up with that money."

"Wait, wait," she pleaded, "you ain't got to do nothing. If there was any money here, I'd have given it to you when I told you where the dope was."

"Goddamn it, bitch," Tree cursed, "we don't want no story. We want the cash, nothing else." He slapped her across the face, then added, "Either give it up or pay the consequences."

Whatever they were going to do, she reasoned, they'd do whether she gave up the money or not. "I tell you," she cried out, "I gave you everything I had when I told you where the stuff was. Please, don't you understand, I just don't have anything. Wait, wait," she added, "I might have twenty dollars or so in my pocketbook, but that's all the money I have to live on until payday."

"I believe her," Tree's partner said. "I don't think they have any bread, man."

Tree shrugged his shoulders as he stared at her young body. "Fuck it!" he exclaimed, then reached down and ripped her nightgown completely off. He stared at her young ripe body. "I want some of this young pussy anyway."

George managed to mutter something for the first time since they entered the place.

Tree turned on him in anger. "Fuck you, punk. The bitch ain't goin' tell the police nothing. If she gets fucked, she just gets fucked, and that's it. What she goin' say? We come in and robbed her of her dope then fucked her?"

"It's rape, man, it's rape!" George finally stated loudly. "I didn't get into this shit for no pussy, man. Fuck that shit. I got all the cock I know how to handle at home."

"Well, go home and fuck it then," Tree replied coldly. "Hey Fred, cook up one of them bags of dope, man. If we goin' to trim the young sister, we might as well make it good to her. Ain't no sense in us coming too soon," he said, and both the men burst out laughing.

Fred slowly removed the outfit and cooker from his

sock. He bit off the end of one of the balloons but found another knot in the balloon. After biting that one off, he dumped part of the dope in the cooker.

"Don't put too much of that stuff in the cooker. It's good dope that ain't been cut to death, Fred. Plus, man, we want to be able to get the old bone hard enough to please Miss Lady."

Sandra stared around wildly. She knew now that the men intended to rape her. She opened her mouth to scream, but Tree caught her in time. He jammed his hand over her mouth, then removed a dirty hankie from his pocket and stuck it down her throat.

"George," Tree said sharply, "get off your trembling ass and help us. Get in the bedroom and find me a sheet so that we can tie this bitch up. I believe she might just put up too much of a struggle. We don't want no noise, you know."

"Man, I want to leave," George stated. "I didn't have any idea ya was going to get pussy struck. Dopefiends, too."

"Well, you ain't going nowhere," Tree answered shortly. "I ain't had no young pussy like this in quite a while," he added, as he reached down and rubbed her leg.

Without thinking, Sandra kicked out and caught Tree in the chest. The blow had been so swift that it took him by complete surprise. He tumbled over on his back. Like a cat she was on her feet and streaking for the door. She tried to snatch the hankie from her mouth so that she could scream as she frantically snatched at the door. She managed to get the lock off and jerked the door open, only to find that the night chain was still on. Before she could close the door and release the chain, Fred was on her. He struck her from behind. The blow was hard and cruel. As she fell against the door, he whirled her around and hit her with a short right to the jaw. She crumpled up like a rag doll on the floor in front of the door.

When she awoke her feet were tied with strips torn from her sheet. She stared at the two men with fear. They were both nodding from the effects of the dope. For a moment she hoped the dope had taken away their desire for sex.

"Well, well, well. Looks like our littl' old fox has finally awoke. For a minute there, sweetie, I was afraid that Fred here had broken your jaw or something. Although that wouldn't have stopped the show. It might have stopped us from enjoying that mellow young head of yours, though." Tree said this as he came up out of his nod. He got up and crossed the floor, then knelt down beside Sandra.

She turned away from him. Slowly she became aware of his hands, probing, feeling, caressing her body. She caught her breath as his fingers slipped up inside her. He pushed two of them in as deep as they would go. As she closed her eyes to blot out what was happening, she became aware of the fact that now there were four hands fumbling around all over her. Chills raced up and down her spine. Her nerves arched as fear traveled from the top of her head to the bottoms of her feet. It felt like her bones and her flesh were being ripped apart from each other. Her throat went dry and her stomach flipped over as they put their hands up inside of her. She tried to use her tongue to moisten parched lips, while she gulped until it looked like she was strangling.

"You keep opening your mouth like that," Tree said, "and I'm goin' put something in it!"

She lifted her head in defiance as determination and anger overwhelmed her very being. Had they known her, the glare of absolute determination and hatred would have warned them that it wasn't over and wouldn't be over until someone was dead. As she felt the first man's dick penetrate her, the fear that had almost petrified her fled. In its place was a cold, chilling hatred.

"Go on, Fred, put your bone in her mouth while I ride this cock," Tree said, breathing hard as sweat poured down off him onto her young body. The smell of the man almost overcame her as she glanced away from the sneering, slobbering man. His spit was dripping out of the corners of his mouth, and as the drops fell on Sandra she twisted her head away and tried to scream.

Fred glanced down into her eyes and shook his head. "No bet to me, baby. I'll never give this bitch the chance to bite half of my dick off, man."

"Don't worry about it, man," Tree replied. "If the bitch tries to bite, I'll break her goddamn neck," he said seriously.

"Yeah, man, I know you will, but that ain't goin' do my pole no good. The bitch would probably die with it like a bulldog, dedicated to the end. No thank you, Tree, you put your dick in her mouth, and let me do the choking if she bites."

Tree didn't answer as he continued to plunge up and down. "Man, this bitch is laying like a piece of wood," he finally said, then added, "Naw, Fred, I ain't goin' take the chance either, plus the bitch ain't goin' suck it right no way. But I got a better idea." He removed his dick and rolled her over on her stomach. "We just bust this cherry back here. I'll bet the bitch don't lay like no log then. "

Pain exploded in her anus. It felt like her very bowels were on fire. She tried to scream but the hankie only made her gag. She swung her head from side to side wildly. Sandra prayed to die, in her agony. It seemed as if the pain would go on and on, but she bit down on her lips and put up with it. Her tears only excited the two men more. They made animal sounds as they argued over the woman. Tree reached around her and picked her up by her small waist. He pulled her to him roughly as he slobbered on her neck, mouthing words of endearment.

"Aw baby, I know it's good to you," he repeated over and over again, until she passed out from the pain.

6

WHEN SANDRA REGAINED consciousness there was no one in the apartment but her. She stared around dully, then managed to untie her feet. The knots had been loose. She noticed that the color television was gone, but that didn't mean anything. She could always get another one. The pain in her rectum had passed, but she found that she had messed on herself. She got up and went into the bath. After a hot shower she began to feel better physically, but mentally was another matter. What they had done to her was something she would never forget. She stared at her face in the mirror. There would always be a scar from where she had been struck with the gun. There was a long rip on the side of her face that would have to heal. She wondered how she could visit Chink this weekend looking the way she looked. Well, it hadn't been her fault, so she'd go see him just like she was. That way, he'd really know what they'd done. She was undecided as to how much to tell him. Some of what they did was too much to tell anyone. She was too ashamed.

For the next two days she ate, slept, and brooded. Her young mind was fertile for revenge. She knew without a doubt that something would be done, even if it took years of patient waiting.

Saturday morning came, and Sandra took her time in dressing. She used a long bandage to cover the scar, but nothing could conceal her swollen lips. For a minute she debated with herself whether or not she should go. This would be their first visit out in the prison yard at a picnic table. She had fixed the lunch. Fried chicken, a lemon pie, and soft drinks. It would be foolish to let someone else interfere with her and her man's enjoyment. After examining the Fred Astaire pants outfit she wore, she couldn't postpone the visit. She carried the lunch basket outside and set it in the trunk of the late model LTD Ford she had bought.

It took two hours before she pulled into the state prison's camp area. The scene of the trees on the side of the road leading into the compound was a tranquil picture. A house sitting on a hill was a beautiful sight to the outsider, but to the one hundred and twenty men at the camp program it was the house of the lieutenant who had complete control of the men who were confined.

Sandra parked the car and went up the walk like a hurt animal looking for its mate. The questions she had feared from the guards were avoided.

From inside the wing of Chink's building the brothers watched the slim, black girl make her way up the walk. All of the men could see the bandage, but only one of them felt pain. Chink came off his top bunk in a smooth motion. Jimmy, the young brother who stayed under him, walked over.

"That's her, huh?"

Chink didn't bother to reply. His blood had run hot on sight of the bandage and he hadn't really heard his friend's question. From the expression on Chink's face, Jimmy realized that his bunkmate was boiling.

When Sandra reached the office Chink was there waiting for her. He carried the picnic basket to the door for her. One of the officers on duty stood nearby. He had watched the transaction through the window.

Neither spoke to the other. Sandra just smiled brightly at him. After another guard had searched the basket, they were free to go. The policemen glanced at the bandaged up young girl but didn't comment.

Sandra leaned against one of Chink's muscular black arms as they walked together towards the picnic area. She could feel his arm trembling with silent rage. A feeling of complete confidence filled the young black girl as she walked beside her man.

"Who was it?" he asked quietly as he led her to a
tree and spread the blanket she had brought. He knelt,
with an end of the blanket in his hand, at her foot. As
he stared up into her face she could see the pleading
in his eyes for the truth.

Sandra stretched her arms out to Chink, and when
he came up to her he took her in his arms. With her
head on his chest she talked slow at first, in a stut-
tering, shaking voice.

At the tables beside them were children and parents, playing and laughing. There was a holiday mood
around the crowded tables. Prisoners walked back and
forth introducing wives and sweethearts to friends, but
no one came near Sandra and Chink. It was as though
they were all by themselves, on another piece of green
velvet grass.

Jimmy came down the walk with his girlfriend and
a small child. The little boy could hardly walk. He
was the only one who moved near the young couple.
The other black inmates had steered clear of Chink,
not out of fear but out of respect. They knew that if
he wanted to visit, he would.

"Do you think I was wrong in giving the dope to
George, Daddy?" Sandra asked suddenly. She hadn't
been watching his face as she spoke; she would have
seen that Chink's eyes had gone from slits to balls of
pure fire. Death was in his face.

Sandra had spoken quietly for over a half an hour
before she had asked the question. She had told every-

thing, just as it happened. His shirt was wet from her tears as she remembered the pain and brutality of the men. She didn't conceal anything.

Just hearing that someone had struck his woman would have been enough to set him off. Sandra was his first and only love. He was like a caged animal. He wanted to strike out. He would never forgive or forget. The magnitude of what the men did to his woman, and men that he knew he could find, sent a cold deadliness through him that only the shedding of blood could remove.

He knew Tree and his partner on sight, but they didn't know him that well. They had seen him, he knew that, and they knew he sold dope. But they had never done any business together. As Chink thought about it, he knew that they based their nerve on his staying in prison and in time making everybody forget.

"I don't think you did nothin' wrong, honey," Chink said softly. "The only mistake done was by the people who did this," he said and kissed the bandages lightly.

"I'm glad you feel that way about it," she replied quietly.

Sandra glanced up into Chink's face. She saw the wetness on his cheeks and it touched her deeply. Her sorrow was his, and her pain was so close to him that he could almost feel it. "Would you care for some refreshments? I have some cold soft drinks, Daddy."

He nodded his head and watched her move gracefully to the basket. She fixed him a drink and a plate of food and set it beside him. When he noticed her about to close the basket, he said, "Don't close it without fixing yourself something, baby. I want you to sure 'nuff eat plenty, 'cause from here on out, you might be busy. I may be coming home this week."

Sandra sat down beside him and glanced around the compound. There was a softball field at the rear of the buildings, with trees showing in the distance. There was no fence around the prison grounds.

"You'll need a ride." was all she said. There was no question about whether he was wrong or not. If he wanted to come home it was his decision. He was the man and she would follow. She felt as if she was lost without him. She needed a man to love and protect her, and this was her man.

They ate in silence, each deep in private thoughts. She worried now about Chink because she knew he was planning revenge.

The day passed slowly, and though the sun was hot it was cool and peaceful under the tree. They ate and drank and made plans. Chink talked, and Sandra listened.

"That's the main thing, baby. You goin' have to get rid of that car 'cause by now they got the license and everything else," Chink said as he lit a cigarette.

Sandra got a light off his cigarette and leaned back against the tree. "It's strange," she said, "how someone can do something and upset the plans of others. I wanted to save and have a lot of money for you when you came home. Now this."

"Life seems to be that way, baby. There's some things a man can accept, and the others he can't," Chink replied quietly.

A song drifted from someone's radio. It was "Reach Out For Me" by the Four Tops. The couple listened quietly to the words. Yes, they were reaching out for each other.

"As long as the timing is right, there should be no trouble. I'll come out right after count. Give me ten minutes to reach the highway through the woods."

She glanced at her watch. "I won't be late. If I am you'll know something happened that I couldn't help."

"Don't take no chances. Move out. Move to a motel. Stay there. Don't even worry about the stuff there. Maybe get yours, and a few of my clothes, but don't take no chances. Throw us a few things together and get the hell out of there." Chink spoke with emotion. His voice was husky and the worry in it could not be concealed.

Sandra nodded her head in agreement. It was a touching moment for the young girl who had never had anyone love her before. To now have someone really care for her was too much for her to hide and the tears ran down her cheeks unchecked.

"What's wrong, baby?" Chink asked, surprised. "I didn't mean to say anything that would upset you."

"It ain't that, Daddy. It's just the knowing that you really care. That you feel this thing as deeply as I do. Chink, baby, I want you to know that there's nothing under the sun that I wouldn't do for you. Do you believe me ?"

For an answer, Chink held her tightly in his arms. Something was flowing between them then. It was a rare feeling that comes to only a few people in a lifetime. They knew that from then on their lives would be woven together. No matter what hardships life might put in their way, it would be together that they would face them.

Later in the afternoon, Jimmy's little boy slipped away from his parents. He wandered over toward the quiet couple. Sandra put out her arms and caught the young boy.

"Come here, sweetie," she cooed and laughed as the little boy grinned and ran into her arms. She kissed him on his cheek and held him up. For a few minutes she played with the child, and then his parents came running over to take him back.

"Damn, Chink, I'm sorry about that," Jimmy said as he came over with his wife. "The little guy slipped off while we weren't looking "

Chink waved his hand. "Man, that ain't about nothing. I was wonderin' when you was going to come on over and introduce us to your lady."

Jimmy grinned. "Honey," he said, "this is my best friend and bunk partner, Chink. Chink, this is my wife, Shirley."

For a moment Chink was embarrassed. He had never liked making introductions, nor meeting women, but he rose to the occasion. He turned and waved toward his lady, Sandra, who was still holding the child. "This is my lady, Sandra. Why don't you and Shirley sit down and join us for a while. Visiting hours will be over soon, so let's have a littl' set."

"Fine, fine," Jimmy said. He went back and got his blanket and joined the couple. Shirley and Sandra were busy talking when Jimmy finally settled down. The men talked quietly for a while, as the women played with the small boy.

"I wanted to ask a favor of you, Chink," Jimmy began. "My woman don't have no car, man, so she has to catch the bus up here. I was wonderin', man, if she could get a ride back home. You know, carrying the child and all, it's a drag on the fuckin' bus."

"Aw, man, that ain't no favor. The women have probably settled that matter between them already," Chink said easily.

Sandra overheard their conversation. "Yeah, baby, done already made plans for that. Don't worry about it. Jimmy, I got some pie in the basket, and cake, if you should want some. You can also make yourself at home with whatever food you might want. I don't want to carry that mess back home, so fill your stomach up."

"Come on, man," Chink said as he got up. He had noticed that Jimmy's wife hadn't brought a lunch. It would have been too much trouble trying to carry everything on the bus. Jimmy was happy enough that she had shown up

"Shirley," Sandra began, "why don't you fix yourself something to eat, too. I brought plenty of the shit along, so make yourself at home. Don't feel funny. I know you ain't had nothing all day." Before Shirley could say no, Sandra added, "At least fix something for the boy."

Shirley grinned and got up and fixed a plate. The four young adults sat around and laughed and talked until the end of the visiting period. When the bell rang, none of them wanted to bring the beautiful afternoon to an end.

"Damn," Jimmy said sharply, "it seems as if the time just flew by." They sat and watched the other people make their final embrace, pack up, and depart. Slowly Sandra began to gather up the small bundle so that they too could leave. Chink held her close, kissing her on the neck, while Jimmy hugged his wife.

They walked back up the path from the picnic grounds and each man held his woman closely. The little boy trotted to keep up. Chink helped Sandra load the basket in the car trunk.

"Well, baby, I guess this is it. We're allowed to make that one phone call home this week, but the guard stands so close that I won't be able to say anything. If it should be called off, I'll tell you that I'll be expecting you up here the next visiting week. If not, then we'll go on with what I've planned. Thursday evening will be the day," Chink added quietly, so that no one could overhear what he said.

"I understand, honey." Sandra replied just as quietly. "Don't worry about a thing. I'll take care of my end."

"I'm sure you will, baby." Chink answered her quickly. "I'm not worried about you takin' care of what you're supposed to do. Everything should go like clockwork. Blacks don't generally run away from these camps, so they don't watch us too closely. It will be child's play." He kissed her again, then stood back as Shirley got in the car.

Jimmy was holding his child tightly. He kissed the boy on the cheek, then put him in the car. His eyes had a watery glaze about them, but Chink didn't speak of it. He knew what the other man was feeling. Both men wanted to get in the car with the women so bad they could damn near taste it. Visiting was nice, but parting was hell. They knew another week was about to begin, a week filled with dullness, boredom, and the bullshit work the men were given to do.

The two men stood beside each other and watched the car until it faded in the distance. Then they turned and slowly walked back up the path that led to the dormitory. Each man was silent, full of his own thoughts. Before they reached the door Jimmy broke the silence.

"When you leave, man, why don't you take me with you?" he asked quietly.

"Leave! What gives you an idea like that, man? I ain't going nowhere for at least another two years, Jimmy."

"Don't con me, Chink. I know goddamn well you're planning on pulling up from here. Ain't no way you goin' tell me different. It's in your eyes, man. All over your face."

Chink didn't answer right away. He just let his eyes run over the rolling, well kept grass and the trees in the distance. "If I should go, man, I'll pull your coat. But Jimmy, ain't no reason for you to run, man. Once you run, you're going to always be wanted. It don't make sense, Jimmy. I wouldn't want to see you fuck up your life like that."

Jimmy stopped with his hand on the door. "Man, I wouldn't want to go if it wasn't important, but my woman needs me. She ain't gettin' but eighty dollars every two weeks, and it just ain't enough for her to make it on with the kid." He hurried on, before Chink could interrupt. "You see, man, we ain't got no people out here in California. We're both from the South, man, and all her people are back there. If I should run, I'd just get the fuck out of the state, that's all. I ain't did enough for them to really put out an all points bulletin on me. I'm just small potatoes, Chink. I'd go back home and nobody would be the wiser."

"I'll let you know, Jimmy. I'd have to think about it, my man. I really would. This is something that came up out of nowhere, man, so you'll just have to wait until I make up my mind on what's the best thing for me to do." He hesitated, then added, "I'll tell you this much, though. I ain't goin' let nothin', man, nothin' interfere with what I got to do. If possible, I'll take you along, but we'll just have to wait and see."

Later, when the chow bell rang, Chink and Jimmy stayed out of the chow line. They were both too full from the food they had eaten outside. Instead, they went into the playroom, which had two pool tables and one ping-pong table. They shot pool for the next hour, until count time. At count time each man had to be at his bunk, standing in front of it. After the guard passed, they still had to wait until the all clear bell rang. It generally came in minutes after the guard made his round.

Goddamn, Chink, I can't seem to get that visit out of my mind. Let's go into the TV room. Is anything good on tonight?" Jimmy asked quietly.

Chink shrugged his huge shoulders. "I don't keep up with that shit, man, you know that." He still led the way toward the TV room. It was full of inmates, some sitting in the front row saving the best seats for their friends who hadn't got there yet. Chink walked up to the front row. Another inmate had put his jacket on two of the seats.

"Whose jacket?" Chink asked, lifting the coat out of the chair.

"That's mine, man," the brown-skinned brother sitting next to the chairs replied. "Them seats is saved, brother," he added.

"Yeah, I know," Chink answered sharply, as he sat down. "The seats are unsaved now, baby."

"Hey, my man," the inmate yelled. "What you goin' do, man? Just grab the motherfuckin' seat?"

Chink stared at the man coldly. "Listen man, let me pull your coat to something. You use that weak ass shit on these ofay punks or on some of these brothers that don't know no better, but don't run that weak ass shit down to me! These seats belong to the state, man, for any convict's use. Now if your buddies can't get their asses down here in time to get a seat, they just have to find one where they can, you dig what I mean?"

The inmate Chink was talking to glanced nervously around. He saw his two friends enter the television room and gained courage.

"Listen man, I don't want to hear that shit. I told you that the seats were saved. Now if you want to try taking them, why don't you tell the brothers who they belong to about it." He had raised his voice so that his partners could hear the conversation.

By now, all activity in the television room had come to a halt. The men had stopped whispering amongst themselves to hear what was going on in the front row.

The habit of certain inmates saving seats, and generally the best seats, was a sore spot with many of the men. Most of them just overlooked it, because they didn't want any trouble over a seat in the damn television room which would cause them to get a flop at the parole board.

Most of the time Chink didn't bother to come into the television room, so he didn't come in contact with the problem. When he did come in, he generally sat somewhere in the middle rows. But tonight, he felt mean.

He glanced up at the two brothers bearing down on

him, then he turned back to the man sitting next to him. The man was smiling as if he was doing something clever.

Without warning Chink slapped him across the face twice. The blows were so hard that they almost snapped his neck. "Goddamn it, punk," Chink growled, "I ain't for no fuckin' games, boy." He stood up and glared at the two men coming towards him.

Both men stopped as if they had car brakes on their shoe heels. What they saw was danger. Chink's long arms seemed to jerk in their need to strike out at someone. Violence was written all over his face: A man would have had to have been either blind or a fool to not have paid heed to the warning in Chink's expression.

The man Chink slapped continued to sit, waiting to see what his friends would do. It didn't take long for him to realize that they weren't about to enter into the argument.

"What's the deal, Peterson?" Chink asked the closest one of the men.

The man called Peterson just shrugged his shoulders. "Ain't nothin' to it, Chink. I see you and my boy there done had a littl' run in. Don't be too hard on him, Chink, he's a good kid."

"Yeah, I know what you mean," Chink answered, then added, "but punks should stay in their places." He still tried to push it. Chink didn't want to let it go at that. He wanted the body contact of a good fight, but Peterson wasn't having any of it.

He raised his hands in a friendly gesture. "Ain't
nothin' but a misunderstandin', my man. That's all,
just a misunderstanding." Before the words were out
of Peterson's mouth, he had glanced around and seen
two empty seats in another row. He led his friend
towards the empty chairs. He was far from a fool. He
had seen Chink's girlfriend show up with the bandages, and he knew from experience that the man was
boiling for a fight. But Peterson wasn't having any of
it. If he wanted a fight, he reasoned as he sat down
in a chair, it would be with someone other than the
gorilla-looking Chink. The man looked like an ape
and was built like one. No, Peterson considered himself wiser than that.

Jimmy sat quietly beside his friend while everything calmed down. He felt a cold shiver of fear at
the wild swiftness of Chink's attack. He knew in his
heart that he was afraid of the man who he slept under.
Chink was just too unpredictable for him. He could
explode in violence in a moment's notice.

Chink sat in the chair for about five minutes, then
got up. "I think I'm going down to the gym and lift
some weights, Jimmy. If you stay up here and run into
any trouble, just come a runnin', baby, and I'll gladly come back with you and handle it." He spoke loud
enough for just about everyone in the TV room to
hear.

"Okay, Chink," Jimmy replied. "I think I'll just stay
and watch this bullshit on TV." He hesitated, then continued. "I ain't too good with that weightliftin' shit,

you dig?"

Chink reached down and rubbed his friend's head, messing up Jimmy's natural. It was something they did when they kidded around, which was really seldom. "Take care of yourself, Jimmy," he said and walked out of the television room.

7

THE HIGHWAY PASSED by swiftly as Sandra drove back home. There was very little conversation between her and Shirley. When they reached the city limits, Sandra asked her if she would mind riding with her while she picked up some clothes. For some reason she felt better with company along as she parked in the garage. On the ride through the city she had told Shirley a little of what happened, so when Sandra got out of the car, Shirley followed.

It didn't take long for the two women to get the few belongings that Sandra wanted. She packed two bags, and as Shirley watched her pack some of the men's clothes, she remained silent, not asking questions that might be none of her business.

"Well, I guess that just about covers everything," Sandra said as she glanced around for the last time.

"You want to come on over to my place?" Shirley asked.

"Just until I can find me another place," Sandra answered quietly, then led the way out of the apartment.

For the next two days Sandra searched for an apartment. She finally found a furnished one bedroom apartment out on 110th and Budlong, well outside of the Los Angeles district.

Thursday morning was slow for her. She had exchanged cars, trading in hers for an older model. She had wanted to make sure she got something that wouldn't break down on them while out on the highway. Now, with just hours to go, she became nervous. She had moved into her apartment, away from Shirley, so that the other woman wouldn't expect anything. As the hour of departure grew near, she began to gather everything she thought they might need. She counted the money she had got out of the bank. It was fifteen hundred dollars, enough to take them just about anywhere Chink might decide they'd need to go.

Back at the prison compound, Chink made his way to the dining hall. Jimmy tagged along. He had constantly worried Chink about the chance of going along. "Listen man," he continued, as they sat at a table by themselves, "let me just go along as far as the city. I ain't askin' you to take care of me or nothing like that. I just want to get to Los Angeles. I can make it from there."

Chink stared at the man coldly. "Jimmy, if anything should happen, man, I'd hate that you were involved. I'm going all the way, man. All the motherfuckin' way. Ain't nothing goin' stop me. You understand that? Nothin', man!"

"I can dig it!" Jimmy replied shortly. "I'm game to go all the way myself, man."

Going against his better judgment, Chink finally agreed. "Okay, man, but remember, if anything happens, baby, you begged into this shit. I don't want you along, but if you insist, I'll take you along." Chink turned his head and stared out of one of the dining room windows. What could happen? He went over it for the thousandth time. Nothing. It should go smooth and simple. If Sandra was there on time, if the count went off like it should, they would have an hour or possibly two hours before another count. So what could happen? They should be in Los Angeles by then.

There were quite a few ifs involved, but from every angle it still seemed simple. "Okay, Jimmy, be ready after the nine o'clock count. But just remember, man, you wanted this, not me."

Jimmy smiled. In a few hours he'd be with his woman. His heart beat faster. It was all he had thought about for the past few days. He knew Chink wouldn't go and leave him, not if he worried him enough, and that was what he had done. From morning to night, until he had worn the man's patience down. Now

Chink had finally agreed to let him go, and it was going to be tonight.

When they left the dining room, Chink stretched out on his bunk and began to read. Jimmy was too excited for that. He went outside and walked around the compound, staring into the woods that he knew he'd be in sometime that night.

"Johnson!" The sound of his name was called in a harsh and commanding voice. "You keep staring off in the woods like that, and you'll make me think you've got ideas of gettin' a littl' rabbit in you!"

At the sound of his last name, Jimmy almost jumped out of his skin. He turned around to see the guard standing right behind him. He had been so involved in his thoughts that he hadn't even heard the guard come up behind him.

Jimmy grinned and spoke politely. "Hi, Officer Williams. I was just thinkin' about all the times I went huntin' back home in the woods. These remind me of them back home, you know."

The officer nodded his head and walked on around the young prisoner. He wasn't worried. He had never figured it out, but ever since he'd worked at the prison compound no black inmate ever ran away. For some reason, they just didn't run, while the whites were just the opposite. If he had walked up on a white boy gazing through the woods like that, he would have been more than suspicious.

But since it had been a black inmate, he quickly forgot about the matter. Later on that night he would think about it again, but then it would be too late.

Chink got up and took a hot shower to ease his nerves. After the shower he sat on Jimmy's bed and played checkers for a while. The night passed slowly. After the seven o'clock count, the men started racing towards the television room.

Goddamn," Jimmy said again, "this waitin' is sure 'nuff bad shit!"

"Be cool, man, just be cool. Time goin' have to pass, so just be cool," Chink cautioned, but he knew how the man felt. Eight o'clock finally came. Just one more hour, Chink told himself. By now, Sandra should already be on the highway. He stretched out on his bunk and imagined her driving down the highway. He thought about Jimmy asking him about Sandra picking them up, and his refusal to admit she was the one. For some reason, one he couldn't explain to himself, he hadn't wanted to bring her name into it. Jimmy would find out soon enough who was picking them up. Until then, let him guess.

Finally the bell rang for the nine o'clock count. Chink jumped off his bunk and stood beside his bed. The men lined up quickly. There was a good movie on television and they wanted to get back into the television room and see it. The faster they lined up, the quicker the guard would take count. But the officer passed by slowly, checking off each name as he went past.

Chink returned to his bunk, but only leaned on it. Jimmy's face was lit with excitement as he glanced

at his partner. Chink waved his hand for Jimmy to be
cool, not to act too impatient. As soon as the guard
walked out of their wing the all clear bell rang. Chink
smiled. So far so good. At least they wouldn't be held
up while the guard made a second count.

As though he had all the time in the world, Chink
opened his locker and took out a small flashlight. He
had had one of the prisoners on work release bring it
back from town. He slipped it in his pocket, then led
the way down the corridor to the dining room. All the
doors in the place were locked as soon as it became
dark. Chink slipped inside the dark dining room and
closed the door quickly after Jimmy came through.
He held his finger to his mouth so that Jimmy
wouldn't speak. He didn't want to take a chance on
anyone in the kitchen hearing them. Sometimes the
night cook would be on duty.

A sharp sound of someone dropping a pot made
him thankful he had been careful. The men moved
silently across the room. Chink tried a window, then
slowly began to open it. After he got the window
open, he beckoned to Jimmy to go on through. He
waited while Jimmy climbed out, then let himself out
and closed the window.

Jimmy led off, running for the woods. Chink cursed
under his breath as he tried to catch up with the slim,
streaking figure in front of him. Jimmy was entering
the woods at the wrong point. This way they'd have
to travel through too much of the woods.

"Slow down, goddamn it," Chink yelled as loud as

he dared. Jimmy waited for Chink to catch up.

"What's wrong, man. I know you didn't want to be fuckin' around crossing the baseball diamond. Anybody could have glanced out of one of the dormitory windows and seen us if we fucked around," Jimmy explained as soon as Chink reached him.

"I wasn't going this way, man. I was goin' creep around past the office and stay in the shadows until I reached the fuckin' highway. Now, we got to go through these fuckin' woods to reach the highway," Chink stated.

"Don't worry about it," Jimmy replied. "I know my way around the goddamn woods, so don't let it bother you. I'll bring us right out where you wanted to be, and we won't be behind your time schedule."

Before Chink could complain, Jimmy led off at a fast dog trot. Chink had to trot to keep up, and he still was behind. A branch caught his jacket and he had to stop. The sound of a dog barking ahead put him on his guard He went forward quietly, moving like a shadow.

Suddenly Chink heard voices in front of him. He crept forward, moving through the woods as if he were one of the night animals whose life depended on caution. As he parted some bushes and glanced out, he saw Jimmy pinpointed in the beam of a flashlight. A farmer held a shotgun on him. In a flash Chink realized what had happened. Jimmy, running straight ahead, had burst out of the bushes on top of a farmer out doing some coon hunting. For a minute, Chink thought about slipping around them, going on to the highway and catching his ride. If it had gone like he planned, none of this shit would have happened. Now Jimmy was in trouble.

Suddenly the farmer's voice came to him in the bush. "By God, I set out to coon hunt tonight, and I sure done caught me a coon, too!" The farmer's cold laugh sent a dangerous chill down Chink's spine, and a cold rage overcame him. He knew now that he couldn't allow his friend to stay in the man's cruel grasp. The sound of the farmer's voice aroused all the contained fury in his soul.

Suddenly one of the dogs began to growl near him. Chink knew that he didn't have a choice in the matter anymore. He had to strike and strike as fast as possible. He burst from the bush like a small black bear, moving like a streak. The farmer's dogs set up a wild commotion but it was too late. The farmer whirled, bringing up the shotgun.

Chink grabbed the barrel of the gun and snatched it toward him, pulling the farmer off balance. As soon as Chink had the gun in his hands, he struck with the stock, catching the farmer flush in the face. He struck again, an unnecessary blow. Teeth and blood flew everywhere. The dogs barked at his heels, yet none of them had the courage to bite him. He turned the shotgun on them and cut loose with both barrels, killing three of the dogs at once. The rest of the pack bolted for the woods.

Jimmy stared down at the farmer as if in a trance.

"Goddamn, Chink, you done killed him," he said in awe. His face was flushed and fear was in his eyes. "Man, the sonofabitch is dead, Chink. What we goin' do, man? I didn't plan on no murder."

Chink stared at Jimmy. He wished he had saved a load of shot from the shotgun so he could have cut Jimmy down. The nigger was shittin' in his pants. Chink made up his mind quickly. "Listen, man, you can still get out of this shit. Ain't nobody missed us yet. All you got to do is go back and keep your mouth shut. In the morning when they start talkin' about the rumors, you act like it's the first time you heard anything about it and you'll be all right." Chink wiped the sweat off his brow. He couldn't go back. He had a debt to pay, and nothing would come between him and that debt.

Jimmy looked at him in wonder. "You sure, man? I mean you don't mind if I get from under it like that? I'd hate to pull out on you, Chink, but murder, man…, I just didn't think nothing like this would happen."

Chink glanced down at the dead white man at his feet before he could reply. He hadn't planned on no murder either. There wouldn't have been one if he had come by himself, but he didn't mention it. What had happened had happened. Nothing could change it. The white man was dead, so be it. It wasn't going to stop him from finding them niggers who raped his woman; that he was sure of.

"You do what you want to do," Chink said. "I got a ride to catch. I don't want my man to be out on the highway waitin' and I don't show up." It would be better not to let this fool know that Sandra was the one picking him up, Chink decided again.

He set off through the woods, not bothering to look back. Chink didn't even bother to wave good-bye. He didn't really trust himself in Jimmy's company. He was too tempted to kill the man.

Jimmy watched Chink disappear into the woods. For a moment he wanted to follow, but something warned him that that would be the foolish thing to do. He'd better get back to the camp grounds as fast as possible and get this murder rap off his back. Once he made count, it would be Chink's case, no matter what Chink said later on.

After leaving Jimmy, Chink made a bee-line straight for the highway. He reached it out of breath, and he stayed in the bush until he saw a car coming slowly down the highway. He took the small flashlight out of his pocket and blinked it twice. The car suddenly picked up speed. It came to a fast stop right in front of the bushes.

Sandra reached over and opened the door as Chink ran from the bushes. He jumped in quickly. "Let's get the hell out of here," he said harshly, breathing hard.

She stepped down on the gas, glancing in her mirror to see if there was any traffic behind them. "Did everything go as smooth as you planned?" she asked quietly.

He slowly shook his head, then explained to her what had happened. "It just goes to show, baby, that you can't do somebody else a favor. Now I got a fuckin' murder charge against me, while that bastard is back at the camp making sure his ass is safe. If I hadn't drug his sorry ass along, none of that shit would have happened."

"What will happen if he got busted on the way back?" she inquired quickly.

"If that happens, baby, you can bet there will be a roadblock ahead of us somewhere, 'cause the moth-erfucker ain't about to keep his mouth shut. No, baby, if that nigger gets caught, it's all up for us.

For a few minutes Sandra was silent, thinking over what her man had said "Baby, you think I should get off the highway just in case something happened?"

"Naw! If we get off the highway, we won't know where we're at. Fuckin' around in any of these small towns around here is trouble. I think our best bet is to stick to the hghway and hope for the best. This is the fastest route back to the city, so just keep your foot on the gas. Just don't go fast enough for the Highway Patrol to stop us. I still got these fuckin' prison clothes on."

She pointed over her shoulder. "All you got to do is climb back there in the backseat. I'm sure you'll find something that will fit you a lot better than that shit you got on." She grinned as he smiled at her for the first time since entering the car.

Chink quickly climbed in the backseat and changed clothes. When he finished, he let down the window and tossed the prison clothes out, shoes and all.

"I feel like a new man now," he said as he climbed back up front. "Damn it feels good just to have on some decent rags, baby."

Sandra glanced at the speedometer, then took her foot off the gas pedal. She had been doing close to a hundred. "This car sure has a lot of pep," she said, trying to say something lightly, to take his mind off his worries

"Yeah, heavy foot," he said as he slid over beside her. "Just keep it on eighty, baby. That will be fast enough." He leaned over and kissed her neck, then smelled the perfume she was wearing. "Damn, baby, that sure smells nice. Always wear it."

Silence fell on the couple in the car. They drove through the night, and when they reached the city limits, Chink spoke to Sandra quietly. "Honey, I don't never want to go back alive, since I know they'll never let me out. I couldn't do life in prison. I just couldn't stand it, you understand. It ain't for me, baby. I'm goin' hold court in the streets, wherever they stop me. That's goin' be my court day, you hear?"

She glanced at him. "I hear, and I understand, Daddy. I don't think I could stand seeing you behind bars for the rest of your life, either. I mean it, Chink, I just couldn't stand the thought of you being there because of me. None of this would have happened if it wasn't for me, Daddy. I realize that, so I'm with you to the end. If it ain't but a day, or a month, or a year. Whatever it is, we're together, honey."

For Chink, just the words she said were enough to

make everything worthwhile. No matter what time he had, he had the love of a woman, one who loved him as much as he loved her. He glanced at her bandaged face and remembered his obligation. It would be paid, no matter what it cost.

"I got us an apartment out on 110th, Daddy. Should we go there now?" Sandra inquired as they came up off the freeway.

"Uh uh, baby. Did you get that other thing I told you about?" he asked.

"It's in the glove compartment, Chink. But shouldn't we go home and rest first, Daddy?"

"No, baby, in the morning half the city will know I'm out. We got plenty business to take care of tonight," he stated as he removed the pistol from the glove compartment. He examined the gun closely. It was a good one, a thirty-eight police special.

"Take me to 51st and Western, baby. I want to pay my friend George a visit before he finds out I'm home and hides somewhere in a hole like the rat he really is."

She didn't bother to argue. He had made up his mind, so all she had to do was follow his wishes. She parked in front of the apartment building he pointed out.

As Chink got out of the car, she asked, "Should I come along, Daddy?"

Chink shook his head. "Naw, baby. You don't need to come. Just as long as you know I'll handle it, that's good enough," he said and closed the car door. Chink was not like other men. He didn't need the company of another person to help him find the nerve to do something unpleasant. He knew what he had to do and went about doing it, without asking help from anyone.

He made his way up to the second floor and knocked on the apartment door. "Who is it?" came the inquiring voice of a woman.

"Is George home, honey? Tell him the man with the bag is here. I want ya to test some stuff for me," he said, and before the words were out of his mouth, the door was opening.

As Chink barged in, the woman stepped back in surprise, her hand flying to her mouth. "That's right, baby. It's me, Chink. Looks like you know that punk you got done did me wrong, don't you?"

George came out of the bedroom wearing nothing but his shorts. "What the fuck's going on in here?" he asked sharply, but as soon as he saw Chink he started to back up.

"Just freeze right there, punk," Chink ordered harshly. He waved his gun at George's woman. "You find a chair and sit down in it," he ordered, and the woman quickly followed his command.

George came out of the bedroom, explaining. "They made me do it, Chink. They made me. They come by here to cop, man, and stuck me up. Then they forced me to take them over to Sandra's house. I didn't want to do it, man, but they made me. You can understand that, can't you. I tried, I mean I really tried. And when they started that shit with Sandra, I really tried to stop them. Didn't she tell you I didn't want no parts of it, man? No parts of it!"

Chink just stared at him. "I want you to tell me just what they did to my woman, and if you let anything out, I'll know, 'cause she already told me what happened. I just want to see how close to the truth you can come," Chink ordered.

George came into the room and sat down on the floor. He began to talk, and as he talked, the tighter Chink's jaw became. Sandra had told him everything except the sodomy part. She had kept that back, mostly because she was ashamed of what had been done to her.

Chink could hardly trust his voice to ask, "Don't that nigger Tree still stay over on 41st, near Hoover?"

George shook his head. "Naw, Chink, he moved over to Ninth Avenue, apartment 10. He stays there with his sister. She's got three kids and gets a check every month. She's scared to death of him, so she can't put him out."

"And his partner, Fred, what about his home life?" Chink asked quietly.

George wiped the sweat off his brow. He was going to get out of it yet, he believed. Chink wasn't really mad at him, he just wanted Tree and Fred. After all, they were the ones who did it. He hadn't done anything and hadn't got a thing out of it, except for the one balloon.

"Fred stays with his mother over on Van Ness." He

hesitated for a moment, trying to think. "It's the house right next to the alley. You shouldn't have any trouble finding it."

George grinned at Chink as if they were partners. "If you should miss Fred at home, man, he's always up to the pool room near the mug on Western. You can't help but to find him at one of the spots."

George's woman looked at him and turned up her nose. Chink didn't miss the action. "What's wrong, missy," Chink asked. "You don't like to hear your man snitch like that?"

She looked at Chink. "If he was a man he wouldn't have told you anything," she said, safe in the belief that nothing was going to happen to her. She hadn't been involved, even though she had helped talk George into getting Tree's help in taking off the robbery. Tree had given her two balloons for her own, but it hadn't been what she had hoped to get.

The first bullet caught her high in the chest and the second one split her nose wide open. George just sat and stared, dumbfounded. He couldn't believe that Chink had shot his woman. And then death was on him before he realized it.

Chink had put the gun up. With his strong hands he reached down and gripped George's thin neck. The smaller man was like a child in his hands. He struggled but it was all in vain. Chink held him at arms length and slowly choked him to death. It was a slow death, as the man kicked and wiggled, but Chink never stopped the pressure.

When he stepped out of the apartment, people were standing in the hallway. The gunshot noise had drawn them out of their filthy, roach-infested apartments to stare in wonder. Violence was not new to them, but it was always interesting. It would give them something to talk about the rest of the week.

Chink brushed past them as if they weren't even there. The people stood in the hall and watched him walk away. No one tried to stop him. There was something about him that put fear in them. He never glanced one way or the other.

8

WHEN CHINK GOT OUT of the car, Sandra sat silently waiting. Once she got out and walked up to the corner. On the way back she heard the gunshots coming from the apartment building. The noise hadn't been too loud. Some people might mistake it for a car backfiring but she knew better. She hurried to the car and got the motor running.

When Chink came out of the building, walking as if he had all the time in the world, she glanced uneasily up and down the streets. Nobody was paying any attention to them. She pulled away just as soon as he got in.

"Hey, baby, what's your rush?" he said and

grinned at her.

Sandra didn't answer, but she continued to drive. She took Normandie Street straight out towards 110th, cutting in and out of traffic all the while.

"Take it easy, momma. The only thing that will get us busted is your driving. Don't get stopped now. Everything is cool." He glanced at her to see if she was shook up. She didn't appear to be too nervous, just excited.

"Did everything go all right, honey?" she finally got around to asking.

"Yeah, baby, everything went just fine. Our friend George won't be settin' up anybody else, unless it's in hell," Chink stated, then laughed loudly. "Just where in the hell are you taking me, anyway?" he asked suddenly.

"Home!" she exclaimed shortly. "I don't care what you say, either. We're going home and have a few minutes to ourselves, Daddy." Her hand dropped down on his lap. If her words hadn't clinched it, her actions did.

Sandra was the first woman who had ever given herself to Chink. She had been a virgin, and he had never forgotten it. The thought of her in his arms was enough to set his mind aflame. He had laid in the county jail too many nights remembering her. Now, it was going to come true again. He could hardly wait. It was as though he was a young kid getting ready to go on a honeymoon. He looked forward to it with excitement.

After Sandra parked, he almost carried her across the parking lot in his hurry. She smiled in the dark as she felt his strong arms around her. How nice it was to be wanted and to be with the one you wanted. "It's been so long, Daddy," she murmured in his ear.

"It won't be long now!" he exclaimed and helped her to unlock the door. They stood inside the door and kissed. It was a long passionate kiss, one that held all their hopes and fears. It was as if they realized that their love would be brief, that time was against them, and they had to live for the moment.

"Honey, can I fix you something? Anything?" she asked in a husky voice.

Chink stared down into the deep black eyes that looked up at him with such affection. His heart skipped a beat. How, what could he do to show this lovely child of God that her love was returned a thousand times over?

"Fix nothing, baby. Just let me hold you close. What could I possibly want other than you?" They kissed again and Chink carried her into the bedroom. Once there, he began to undress her slowly. Each piece of clothing came off with loving care. Sandra lay back against the soft sheets and held her arms open for him.

Her embrace was like a hot burning fire, and he was consumed in the flames of her heat. He cried out once, then threw himself back into the consuming fire. They lay in each other's arms later, resting. The night was theirs, and no one could take it from them.

Sandra held him close and wondered how many more nights like this would she be allowed. She trembled slightly as she thought of the answer.

Later, after Sandra had drifted off to sleep, Chink lay awake and stared at the ceiling. This was the best time in the world for him to strike. Very few people knew he was out. The ones who counted, anyway. The people he had to reach could only be reached as long as they didn't know he was home, but once they found out he was loose, they'd go in hiding.

Chink got out of bed slowly, not wanting to disturb his woman. He dressed in the dark, then went to Sandra's purse and got the car keys. It would be best to leave her home. The less she was involved, the better. He removed the pistol and broke it open. There weren't but four shells left. He opened up the dresser and searched but couldn't find any more shells. More than likely, he assumed, the six that came with the gun were all she had.

He grinned in the dark. It was just like a woman, he thought as he stuffed some money into his pocket. Chink walked back over to the bed and glanced down at Sandra. He wanted to lean down and kiss the tender lips, and all at once he was overcome with a longing that shook him all the way down to his toes. It was a desire to hold her so tight, to keep all the hardships in life away from her. Oh, if he only could, how sweet it would be.

Suddenly her eyes opened and she stared up at him. The first thing she did was smile. "Hi there. Don't tell me you were planning on leaving me?" she inquired softly.

"You've been laying there faking it, woman. How long have you been awake?"

"Oh, I don't really know, honey. Should we try and go back to the moment that you first got out of bed. You looked so cute searching around in the dark that I couldn't spoil your fun for you, now could I?" Sandra asked.

Chink laughed. "Well, I guess you couldn't. Now that you're awake, or rather, now that I know that you're awake, how about lettin' me know if there are any shells around anywhere. I hope you bought more than just the six that came with the gun."

Sandra shook her head. "No, Daddy, I'm sorry about that. The nigger I got the gun from didn't have any more shells, so I got what I could." She looked away from him, not wanting to see his eyes. For a moment she felt as if she had let him down. How stupid of her. She should have realized that he would need more than just six bullets, but it had escaped her mind for some reason.

"Hey there, doll. We ain't goin' have long faces now. That won't do at all. It's nothing, Sandra. Anybody would have did the same thing. Gettin' the gun was the big thing, baby. Pickin' me up was the big thing, baby, so don't let such a small thing as not having bought enough shells disturb you whatsoever, hear?" He gave her a big squeeze. She slipped her arms around his neck and tried to pull him back into the bed.

Chink laughed pleasantly. "You make me feel so good, momma. I mean it! I've never felt the way I feel when I'm near you." He kissed her slowly, then removed her arms from around his neck. "Honey, I've got business to take care of. If I stay anywhere near you, I'll forget about it."

"Daddy, I was wonderin', can't it wait until tomorrow, or next week, or next month for that matter? I mean, if we just stay here out of sight, Chink, ain't nobody goin' come around, 'cause don't nobody know I stay here. I didn't even let Jimmy's wife know where this place is, so we ain't got no worry. We still got money in the bank, so we ain't worried about cash for the time being."

"Sandra, honey, just stop and think for a minute." He reached up and patted the bandage on the side of her face. "This is the reason why I came home, baby. I love layin' up with you, ain't no doubt about that. But this is our number one concern. Makin' sure them niggers pay. So far, we ain't did nothin'. That punk, he didn't even count. The motherfucker I want is Tree, and I'm planning on havin' him or his partner some time this morning."

"I'm sorry, Daddy. I hadn't forgotten, but it was so beautiful just havin' you home with me that I'd forget everything in my desire to keep you near. Can you understand where I'm coming from? I just want you." With that she pressed her head to his chest and sobbed quietly.

"Hey, hey, baby, what's all this shit? Don't do that

to me. Dry up them tears, honey, and everything is goin' be all right." He kissed her gently, then laid her back on the bed. He glanced at the clock. "It's six o'clock, Sandra. I was waitin' for this time of the mornin', honey. People are gettin' up and going to work, so I won't be too conspicuous. I can move around fairly well this early without too much trouble."

"Why don't you let me go with you then?" she asked. Her voice was strong now; there were no signs of tears anymore.

"Honey, I'd love nothing better, but as I said, if I move by myself, I'm not conspicuous this early in the morning. But if I have you with me, well, we both become something other than a poor nigger trying to make it to work. You're too young lookin', first of all. They might just stop me out of curiosity, wonderin' what the fuck am I doing with such a young girl out at such an hour." He grinned at her, taking the sting out of his words. "Baby face," he said, teasing her, "that's what you get for lookin' so tender." He kissed her again, then became serious. "But don't worry, honey. I'll just knock off one of them motherfuckers, then come running home, okay?"

Chink finally made his escape from his woman. He smiled in the morning darkness as he opened the door to the car. Sandra didn't realize just how tempted he had been to accept her offer of just laying up with her for about a month. After this shit was over, he'd do just that. Go into hiding, stay in the bed and watch television for a month or two. By then the heat should be off, making his escape more easy. He realized that by now the police probably had an APB out on him.

The big car drove smoothly and for the moment he just sat back and enjoyed the ride. Chink made sure that he stayed within the speed limit. When he reached Western and 68th Avenue, he saw a black and white police car. They turned in behind him, making his heart beat faster. He felt the gun in his waistband. It gave him a feeling of comfort. He knew they'd never take him easy. If they had any thoughts on the matter it had better be on holding court in the street, because that was the way he was going to play it.

When he reached Manchester and Western, the police car turned off. Chink gave a sigh of relief. He wasn't frightened of the police, but he didn't want any trouble with them. Not yet, anyway. Not until after he had paid off his debt. Then, whatever happened, it would be all right with him. Chink spotted another police car and a curse exploded from him. The second police car made up his mind for him. He had wanted to find Tree, but since Fred lived close to where he was at, he decided to stop by and pay Fred a visit.

He pulled up and parked two doors away from the house next to the alley. He got out and walked back up the street. Chink stopped and checked the address. It matched the one he had. He strolled up to the door and knocked. It took a second heavy knock, then a wait of a few minutes before an angry woman came to the door.

She glared out the screen door at him. "What could you possibly want, young man, at this hour of the morning?" she inquired, as she pulled her wrapper tighter around her large waist. Chink could see the huge tits trying to bust out from under the ragged gown the woman wore.

"I'm sorry, ma'am, but you see, I was supposed to stop by and pick Fred up this mornin'. He asked me if I could get a job for him out where I work." He stopped to see how she was taking it. The sound of job had done the trick because the woman smiled at him and opened the screen door.

"Well, come on in then. Fred's got his ass in the bed, but I'll sure as hell get him out of there if a job's involved."

Chink followed her into the living room. "You ain't got to go to no trouble, ma'am, I'll go wake him up if you'll just point out where he sleeps. That way you can go on back to bed and get your rest, or fix yourself some coffee or something. I'm just sorry that I had to wake you up, but since my boss told me to bring him in today, I just had to let him know that here was his chance."

Fred's mother glanced at Chink and smiled. My God, she said to herself, he's ugly, but he seems so nice. That's generally the way it is, though. Find somebody born lookin' like that, and they turn out to have the nicest personality.

"I'll tell you what," she said, turning and facing

Chink direct, "you go on in his bedroom and wake him up. By the time he's up, I'll have some hot coffee for both of you. How about that?"

Chink smiled at her. "Missus, now don't you go to no trouble now, you ain't got to put yourself out for me. I'd appreciate some coffee, but I don't want you to go through no trouble."

She grinned, pleased with herself. "Now don't you worry about that. It ain't no problem. I was goin' fix myself a potful anyway, so addin' a littl' mor' water ain't no trouble at all." She raised her hand and pointed out a bedroom. "That's where you'll find that lazy nigger. If he acts like he don't want to go, you just yell out for me. He better not turn this job down. I mean, he just better not, if he wants a roof over his head. I'm tired of Fred's shit, if you know what I mean."

Chink shook his head in agreement. "I know just what you mean, but you won't have to worry after today," he said sharply, then turned on his heels and walked towards the bedroom. He didn't bother to knock. He let himself in and closed the door behind him.

For a brief minute, Chink just stared down at the sleeping form. As he glanced away from the sleeping man and examined the room, he could feel the hatred building up in him. He remembered George's words, as he retold the rape. A blind rage overcame him, and he put the pistol back in his pocket and reached down and slapped the man awake. The cluttered up bedroom disappeared. Now there was only Chink and the man struggling under his fingers, which were now bands of steel. Each finger seemed to be buried somewhere inside the man's neck, because they couldn't be seen on top of Fred's neck.

Fred was a different sort of man than George, though. He was wide awake now and struggling for his life. He kicked out, trying to get his feet free from the bedding, but his struggles were useless. Had he been wide awake, Chink might have met his match, but the man was at a disadvantage. When he awoke, Chink had already gotten his strangle hold.

"Do you remember Sandra, nigger? Do you! That's right," Chink said as he saw understanding come into the fear-ridden eyes. "That's right, nigger, I'm her man! I know you're sorry, but didn't you enjoy that pussy, man. Didn't you? You should have, 'cause you're going to die for it. Was it worth it, nigger? Was it worth it?" Chink spoke in a low voice. The words could hardly be heard by the struggling man, if he bothered to pay any attention to them. He tried to break the grip, the fingers just seemed to bury themselves that much deeper. Slowly Fred's feeble struggles came to a halt, but the man applying the death grip never let up. When the man on the bed changed color, the man doing the choking only added more power. He squeezed until life was gone, until the soul had departed, yet he retained his grip. Tears ran down his cheeks, but it wasn't for the man he had killed. He was picturing his woman under the brutal attack of the man he had killed.

Chink glanced around the room and saw a switch-blade knife lying on the night stand next to Fred's wallet. He released his grip and picked up the knife. Slowly he cut the dead man's throat. After doing that, he took the knife and plunged it down into the life-less form's chest.

Slowly Chink shook his head. He cleared his eyes and slowly walked to the door. He opened it and glanced out. He could hear noise coming from the kitchen. For some reason, he had liked the woman who had let him in, so he didn't want to hurt her. He slipped out of the bedroom and tiptoed to the front door. He let himself out quietly, closing the door behind his departure.

After reaching the sidewalk, Chink walked faster. He didn't want the woman to glance out and see what kind of car he was driving. He opened the door and got in. Quickly he started the motor and pulled away from the curb.

The first corner he came to, Chink turned and drove towards Western. One down and one to go. If he moved fast enough, it should be done before the morning was over. His debt would be paid.

9

BACK AT THE PRISON compound, the morning found the place in an uproar. Rumors flew back and forth between the men confined there. Chink's disappearance had been discovered an hour after he had departed. The body in the woods had been discovered by the farmer's son, some time before four o'clock in the morning. The son, not too happy about his mother waking him up to go look for his father, had found the dogs inside the yard as soon as he came out of the farmhouse, so he knew at once something was wrong. After backtracking, he had found his father's body. Then he notified the Highway Patrol. The first thing they told him was that a convict had escaped.

As soon as the count came up wrong, the Highway
Patrol had been notified to be on the lookout for one
black inmate.

Later, when daylight came and they examined the
grounds, the farmer's son had been the one to find
two sets of tracks. One led toward the highway, the
other led back to the prison compound. For a while
the officers stood around discussing the strange
arrangement, until the captain showed up.

"It's simple as hell," he had growled. "One bastard
got cold feet and ran like hell back to the compound."
He glared around at the other officers. He watched
them shake their heads in agreement.

"I think we better root the bastard out, right quick,"
he ordered sharply.

"How do we go about that little old thing?" the
night sergeant asked. He was already mad because it
had happened on his shift. Now that it was becoming
clear that it was two runners instead of one, he was
in a hurry to get hold of the one that had stayed
behind.

The captain didn't even bother to answer. He whispered with the lieutenant who was in charge of the
Highway Patrol. They walked over to his car and sat
down, talking together. The other officers glanced at
each other sheepishly. They couldn't do anything until
after their superior officer came back and gave them
an order.

"I wonder what the hell they're up to?" one of the
deputies asked a guard standing next to him.

The guard shrugged his shoulders. "It beats the hell out of me. I'd think they'd be for rushing back to the compound and talking to each sonofabitch locked up there. Somebody knows something, and somebody will talk."

"I was always under the impression that those guys were pretty close-mouthed," the deputy said, talking just to kill time.

"That's the coldest shit in town, or else some of that shit you see on television," the guard answered quickly, glad to display his knowledge. Other officers had gathered around the two talking men, listening. "Them fuckin' punks up there would snitch on their mothers if they thought it would get them a few days off. Yeah, that's all the captain's got to do; just go back to the compound and let it be known that whoever comes forward with the information that will help in this case, he'll get maybe a month or two off his sentence. And I'll bet within an hour we'll have the other bastard."

Another guard shook his head in agreement. "You better believe it. John's damn right about that."

"Well, I wish the hell something would happen," another highway patrolman stated. "I'm tired of these fuckin' bugs that keep flying around in these woods. It seems as if they've taken a personal liking for me," he said as he slapped at his cheek, trying to kill one of the millions of gnats that infested the woods.

"Hey," an officer in plain clothes yelled, "don't none of you guys walk over there in that area. We want it clean. Just like the killers left it, not cluttered up by you guys tracking around over there."

The men fell silent as the stretcher bearers came by, carrying the body. The silence held until the men had put the body in the rear of the ambulance and departed.

The farmer's son walked up. "Well, what are these guys going to do? Stand around with their fingers jammed up their asses the rest of the day?"

"Take it easy, kid. Just another few minutes and everything will work itself out. Don't worry, the captain isn't sitting over there talking about the weather, you can bet on it," one of the guards stated, shamed by the man's words.

The young farmer looked at the guard. "And just what the hell were the guards doing last night, to allow these murdering bastards to roam around loose? I thought you guys guarded them punks over there and didn't allow them to walk through the woods like they owned them."

The sergeant glanced up. Hurt was in his eyes. "Listen, son, I understand you're hurt about your father's death, but you and your father have brought prisoners back before just so that you could collect that fifty dollars on them, so you know what's happening over there at the compound. I remember the last time your father was there, the Captain personally warned him about not taking any chances when arresting these guys because some of them could be dangerous."

The sound of another car arriving cut off the farmer's reply. All the men standing in the woods waited silently until the car parked. From where they were, they could see the captain and lieutenant get out of their car and walk over and join the men who had just arrived. They came through the woods together. The new arrivals had two bloodhounds on their leash. The dogs strained to get loose; the smell of blood excited them.

Excitement ran through the crowd of men as they watched the dogs approach. It was just a matter of time now, they knew. Some bastard would be busted before the sun got up in the sky good.

The dog handlers led the dogs over to the tracks leading back to the compound. Quickly the dogs picked up the scent. They started baying at once. Slowly the men set out on the tracks.

The captain waved the sergeant over toward him. "Tom, you rush on back and have the men get ready for count. Have each man at his bunk when we get there."

"Yes, sir!" the sergeant answered sharply, then took off on a slow run. He reached the pickup truck that the state supplied for them. In seconds he was gone in a cloud of dust.

The men followed behind the dogs, and everybody was silent, each man deep in his own thoughts.

The nearer the dogs got to the building, the louder their barks. The men following almost had to run to keep up.

When the sergeant went inside the dormitory, it wasn't necessary for him to explain anything. All he had to do was ring the count bell. The sound of the bell going off set the inmates into motion. They scurried toward their bunks like trained mice.

Jimmy glanced up and down the aisle nervously. He kept telling himself over and over again that he didn't have anything to worry about. But why this unscheduled count? Maybe Chink got busted. If so, did Chink involve him, he wondered over and over again. If he had, all he had to do was deny it. It was just a case of his word against Chink's.

There was a sudden commotion outside. The men nearest the windows craned their necks trying to see. Suddenly the rumor came back down the rock. They had bloodhounds outside. The word filled Jimmy with fear. He hadn't thought about that. Dogs! Bloodhounds! He couldn't believe it. They were wrong.

Suddenly the sound of a hound baying came to all the men inside the building. Jimmy's knees started to shake. He wanted to run, but there was nowhere to run. Oh my God, he cried out suddenly, silently, as he clutched at the bunk for support. It was all over. He knew it. He didn't even glance up when the back door opened and the dogs came in, followed by eight white men.

Before the dogs reached him, they started to strain at the leash. All at once Jimmy couldn't take any more. He knew the dogs were coming straight for him. He broke and ran.

"Stop him!" the captain roared. "Goddamn it, stop him!" His order was followed by the quick work of four prisoners. They wrestled amongst themselves in their hurry to reach him. Jimmy didn't stand a chance. Even if he had gotten past the four inmates who grabbed him, there were more waiting to take the others' place.

The captain walked up, followed by the Highway Patrol officer. "You might as well handcuff the bastard and take him on down to the county jail. See to it, Ed, that the sonofabitch is booked on first degree murder."

"I didn't do it, captain, I swear. It was Chink." The words burst from him. He didn't care if the other men thought he was a snitch. It didn't matter right at that moment, even though, in later life, those very words would end up haunting him to his death. They would brand him as a snitch from that day on.

"Please, captain, please," he begged.

The captain glanced down at the man falling on his knees. It was enough to turn his stomach. He hated informers. Too many of them came through his office, snitching on their friends. He had to use them, because that way he found out about men who were thinking about running. But he hated them.

"Get that sorry sonofabitch out of my sight before I end up puking on him," the captain growled.

The inmates watched silently as Jimmy was carried out of the dormitory. They would think of Jimmy for a long time.

The panic inside Jimmy was finally slowing down.
He could think again. Cold reason was coming to him,
and he started planning. He believed if he turned
state's witness, he would get a break.

By the time the deputies delivered their prisoner to
the county jail, he was a changed person. Gone was
the clinging, begging inmate. In its place was a man
who was determined to sell a friend down the river.
Jimmy had made himself forget that he had begged
Chink to take him along. There was no thought in his
mind that, had he waited and allowed Chink to lead
the way, they wouldn't have run into the farmer. He
was determined to take the witness stand against his
friend.

10

WHEN THE CALL CAME in to the precinct about another murder, this time on Van Ness Street, it was too much of a coincidence for one detective.

Detective Vardis Fisher had been up with the murder case of a man and woman killed in an apartment. The woman had been shot, while the man had been strangled to death. Now another strangling case. When Fisher walked out of the house on Van Ness he was sure of one thing: the killer was the same person. There was no doubt about that. There couldn't be two people who looked like an ape running around killing people. And from all the people he had talked to in the apartment building on Western, the same description kept coming through.

He walked slowly towards his car, followed closely by his colored partner, detective third class Jerry
Horner. Fisher didn't even bother to glance back at
his younger partner. The man just followed along quietly. When they reached the car, Fisher got in on the
passenger side. This was out of the ordinary, because
Fisher generally preferred to do the driving himself.

After both men got settled in the car, Horner broke
the silence. "Well, at least we know it's the same guy
killin' everybody," Horner stated, watching his white
partner out of the corner of his eye. He started the
motor, though not sure where they were going.

"I think we better go on back to the office, Jerry.
Maybe something might have come in to give us a
lead on this madness." Fisher spoke quietly as he
leaned over and lit a cigarette.

Horner just grunted for an answer and followed the
command. His mind was occupied with the murders
too. The men rode in silence until Fisher spoke.

"You know, Jerry, that last guy back there, he was
a pretty good-sized man. Yet his mother hadn't heard
any kind of commotion coming out of the bedroom."
He was talking in a monologue, as if he was rehears-
ing a speech or something. "Yeah, that's the strange
thing about it," Fisher continued. "This guy doing
these killings must have a hell of a lot of confidence
in his own strength. I mean, it takes a certain kind of
man to have the nerve to walk into another man's
home and strangle him to death. I could dig a guy

walking in there and firing away with an automatic, but this strangling shit has got me. I mean, we know the guy's got a gun, unless he got rid of it after shooting that woman. So why didn't he use it instead of this other shit. Maybe he was afraid of making noise, but that wouldn't have made any sense. Not when this same guy walked into a fuckin' apartment building five or six hours earlier and fired away as if he was out on a firing range. Naw, something's wrong here. The mother didn't recognize the picture of the couple who got hit, but yet, we know all three of them were drug users."

Horner added his uh huh and nodded whenever he thought it was time to, but other than that he didn't add anything else to the conversation. He just drove and listened. When they reached headquarters Fisher wondered why there were so many Highway Patrol cars parked.

"Oh that," Horner said, glad for the chance to show that he did know something. "They're probably here because of that escape from the youths' work program camp. I heard something about it just as I was leaving. It seems as if some farmer got killed by the inmate who escaped. It was a brutal killing. He was beat to death with the stock from his shotgun."

Fisher sat up, interested. "From the looks of things," he said, waving at the empty parked cars, "they must have caught the bastard already. These guys don't get off their asses unless they think they're going to get their fuckin' pictures in the paper!"

Slowly Horner backed in and parked. "It seems as if our homicide department is going to get its fair share of action for the weekend," he stated dryly.

"I got a hunch," Fisher began, "that if we don't hurry up and catch the strangler, we're going to get some more action out of that boy. Maybe he's a nut of some kind, I don't know, but I do believe one thing. We ain't heard the last from our busy hatchet man."

The men walked into the building and caught the elevator. The elevator stopped on the third floor and two more detectives got on. They nodded to Horner, but one of them spoke to Fisher.

"Well, if it ain't Fish," a gray-haired officer said. "They keeping you busy, boy?"

Fisher shrugged his shoulders. "Twenty-five hours a day," he replied, then added: "Where are you guys off to this early? I've never seen you off your coffee break this early in my life."

The officer shook some papers in his hand. "It's that fuckin' farmer's case. You know, the one that got killed last night while trying to stop two inmates from escaping." He continued before Fisher could ask any questions. "Well, they caught the one that stayed behind. I'm on my way up to interrogate him, and from what I understand, he's ready to help us all he can. He wants to be a state's witness against his partner who he claims did the killing."

The men laughed. "They all say that," Fisher stated coldly. "Whenever you catch one, it's always the other one who did the killing. Well, good luck with it."

As the elevator stopped on their floor, the other detective spoke up before getting out. "In this case it ain't hard to believe," he stated loudly as he got out. "The sonofabitch that got away looks more like a fuckin' animal to me than anything else. A fuckin' gorilla or something," he yelled back over his shoulder.

Fisher was one step ahead of his partner as he stuck his foot in the elevator door, stopping it from closing. Both men nearly ran out of the elevator.

The other set of detectives stopped in their tracks and stared at the men running toward them. "What's the matter?" the gray-haired one asked in surprise.

"I'm not sure, Al, but it just might be that you've given me the key I need to break open my case," Fisher said seriously.

Horner and Fisher followed Al and his partner into the interrogation room. As they waited for them to bring Jimmy in, Fisher studied the mug shots of Chink.

"Yeah, I can see what they mean," Fisher said, speaking to no one in particular. He held the picture out for Horner to inspect.

Horner shook his head in agreement. The picture of the young boy was bestial to a degree. His hair was uncombed, probably from lying on a hard bunk and being called out to have a mug shot taken.

A turnkey led Jimmy into the room, then departed. Jimmy glanced around nervously. "Sit down, kid. Nobody's going to hurt you here. We just want to hear what you got to say, that's all. Here, have a smoke," the detective called Al said and held out his pack.

Jimmy took one of the cigarettes, then leaned back in his chair.

Al's partner held up a folder. "Well Jimmy," he said, "just start talking and tell us everything from the beginning."

"Hey man," Jimmy said quickly, "I want some kind of understanding, man. Are you guys going to give me a break if I turn over and be a state's witness?"

"Break hell," Al said harshly, coming up from his chair. "Boy, you're implicated in a murder. Now you can talk if you want to, if you think it will help. We'll listen, but as far as a deal, get it out of your mind. We got your ass on murder, and we can try you on first degree if we want to."

Al's partner took it up, coming in with the soft stuff to win Jimmy over. "Now Jimmy, what my partner says is true, but I'll promise you this, and I'm sticking my neck out when I say it, but if you talk and what you say helps us to catch up with your partner, well, I'll personally try and get your charge reduced."

By now, Jimmy was in a cold sweat. He hadn't expected it to go like it was going. He had been sure the officers would offer him a cop. "Man, if I talk and it ain't goin' help me, why what's the use of talking?" He hesitated, then added, "I ain't killed nobody, man. I mean that."

The detectives glanced at each other, then Al's partner took it up. "Well Jimmy, I'll tell you this much.

We got the murder weapon, and it's full of prints. Now
if your prints ain't on it, well boy, you stand a good
chance."

A good chance of what, he didn't say, and Jimmy
didn't bother to ask. The mention of the murder
weapon showed him his way out. He knew he hadn't
left any prints, because he had never touched the gun.
Jimmy started talking, and for the next hour he talked
while the detectives just listened. When Jimmy first
spoke of Chink, Fisher started to interrupt, but he
respected his fellow officers too much for that. He
decided to wait until they had finished questioning
Jimmy, then he could ask his questions.

The interrogation went on for over two hours, then
the detectives prepared a statement and pushed it in
front of Jimmy to sign. He signed without even bothering to see what he was putting his name to. He had
put his confidence completely in the policemen.
Whatever they did, he would have to go along with
now.

"Al, when you finish I'd like to ask him a few personal questions," Fisher said from the sideline.

Al waved his hand magnanimously. "Go ahead,
Fish, we got just about everything we'll need. If we
find we forgot something, we'll know where to pick
him up at." He laughed, as if he had really said something funny.

Fisher walked up to the table and glanced down at
the frightened man. "Jimmy, you said that after Chink
saw his woman on visiting day, he started bugging

you to run away with him."

Jimmy shook his head in agreement. "That's right, man. Like I said, somebody had beat the shit out of her and Chink wanted my help once we got free to help him handle these guys."

Fisher's expression never changed as he stared down into the man's eyes. "Then would you say that Chink would probably be afraid to go up against these guys by himself?"

The question caught Jimmy by surprise. As he closed his eyes and saw Chink, he couldn't imagine the man being afraid of anyone. "Well, I don't know about that, man. To be truthful with you, I don't think Chink is afraid of anything or anybody, man."

"Well, why did you say Chink wanted your help once you two got free then? If he's not frightened, I don't see why in the fuck would he need your help," Fisher stated brutally, finally getting tired of the lies he knew Jimmy was telling.

"Listen, bro," Horner said, speaking for the first time since entering the tiny room. He stepped up to the small table that Jimmy sat in front of. "We don't give a shit why you ran away or what happened, so don't bullshit us. All we're interested in is Chink. Now tell the fuckin' truth! You mentioned that Chink's woman had been beat up. Who did it? What did she look like, and where can we reach her?"

Jimmy glanced up at the colored detective. "I don't know where she stays, man. All she did was give my wife a ride home. As far as what she looked like, she had a large bandage on one side of her face, but that's about all I can tell you, other than her name was Sandra. Oh yeah," he added, as an afterthought, "I think she was busted on his case with him, but she didn't get any time out of it for some reason."

A smile broke across Fisher's face. He patted his partner on the back. "I believe we got something we can go on now," he stated happily.

"Who was it who was supposed to pick you guys up on the highway?" Fisher asked suddenly.

Jimmy shook his head. "I don't know, man. Chink never would say, but I believe it was his woman, 'cause he hadn't planned on running away until the day she came and visited him all beat up."

"What kind of car was she driving?" Al asked sharply.

"It was a Ford, but Chink said something about her gettin' another one, so I figured she was the one who was going to pick us up."

Fisher turned to his partner. "I believe we've gotten all we need from this punk. Let's go and check on women's division. From there we should be able to get a lead on this Sandra. Maybe she's on probation or something." Fisher raised his arm and waved at the other detectives. "Thanks, Al, I think I got what I came for, and more!"

He led the way out of the tiny room. "Jerry, while I'm at women's division, you run up to the probation department and check it out. I'll meet you back at our department as soon as you're finished, okay?"

Horner shook his head in agreement. "Okay, Fisher," he replied, not mentioning what he really wanted to say, which was that they had been on the case since midnight, and it seemed to him that they could turn the fuckin' case over to the day shift and take their asses home. But that wasn't Fisher's way of doing things. He'd run around like a chicken with its head cut off, until he damn near dropped from fatigue.

11

AFTER LEAVING FRED'S house, Chink drove slowly as he planned his next move. He noticed the gas gauge and stopped and filled up the tank. When he pulled out of the gas station he fell in behind all the morning traffic. The cars were bumper to bumper, so it took him a while to reach the east side. He searched out the address, driving down the street slowly, until he came to the apartment building where Tree lived.

He parked, got out, and studied the street carefully before going into the building. The steps were old and creaky and it seemed as if the noise would wake everybody in the building. He grinned as he realized that the people who lived in the building were probably so used to hearing the steps cry out every time someone used them that it was a normal sound to them.

He stopped on the second floor and started searching for the apartment number George had given him. He came to the apartment and stood outside, listening. He could hear sounds coming from the inside. He leaned closer, putting his ear next to the door. He finally figured out that the sounds were made by children.

He knocked sharply on the door. "Who is it?" The question was asked by a woman.

Chink hesitated briefly, then said, "It's Fred, honey. I'm lookin' for Tree."

Suddenly the door was opened widely. Before the woman could close it Chink had stepped inside. She stared at him coldly. "You ain't Fred," she said.

"I don't know what Fred you're talkin' about," Chink replied, "but my name is Fred." He glared at her, then asked harshly, "Where's Tree?"

She seemed to make up her mind all at once. "He's in there," she said and pointed at the bedroom.

At the same time, the bedroom door opened and Tree glanced out. He was still in his shorts. He stared angrily around until he saw Chink, then he ducked back into the bedroom, slamming the door behind him.

His sister stared at the action stupidly. Chink broke into a run and hit the door with his shoulder. The thin bedroom door burst open. Chink fumbled at his waist for the pistol as he fell into the room.

Tree hadn't wasted any time. He had run straight back to his bed and snatched his own pistol out from under the pillow. One look at Chink and he had quickly realized why the man was there. He didn't know how the man had found him and didn't waste any time thinking about it. He came up with his pistol and fired wildly as Chink came tumbling into the room. His first shot hit the wall, but as Chink fumbled with his gun, Tree took his time and fired again. His second shot hit Chink in the stomach, and his third one hit the huge young man somewhere in his wide chest. Neither shot seemed to have any effect on Chink. It was as if he had been programmed to do something and nothing could stop him.

Tree watched with horror as he raised the gun. He started to toss his own gun down and run, but there was nowhere to go but past the man in the doorway. Either that or jump out of the window, and neither idea seemed too good.

Chink fired and the shot took Tree between the eyes. He fell back as if he was clubbed by a giant blow. Chink fired again, then walked over to the fallen body and shot him in the back of the head. He bent down and picked up the pistol Tree had used. He stuck it in his waistband.

As Chink started from the room, he stumbled once, then caught himself and made his way out, walking slowly. Tree's sister stood holding her hand to her mouth, her kids around her. Fear was something she

had known many times before, but as she saw the
expression on the big man's face as he came out of
the bedroom she felt a cold, numbing fear that seemed
to chill her very bones. She couldn't move. She could
only stare wildly and pray that the man wouldn't kill
her and her children. Death was there in his face, but
as she watched him make his slow way, she suddenly realized that if she stayed out of his way he
wouldn't bother them. She clutched the children closer and watched him leave. She stood that way, not
bothering to go to the window to see how he left. She
didn't want to know anything about the man who had
walked in and killed her brother. And she was sure
without even looking in the bedroom that Tree was
dead. Something told her that the man who had just
left wouldn't have left until after Tree was dead.
Whatever Tree had done he had done to the wrong
man.

Chink walked down the steps slowly. He wanted to
just lie down somewhere, but the picture of Sandra
waiting on him came to his mind and he continued
on his way. He finally got down the steps, ignoring
the people who came out of the apartments and stared
at him. Before he reached the outside door, he remembered he still carried his gun in his hand. He stuffed
the pistol down in his waistband next to the one he
had stuck there earlier. The walk to the car was hard-
er than anything he had ever attempted before.
Coming down the steps he had had something to hold
on to, but trying to reach the car was another matter.

There was nothing to balance himself with, and the pain in his stomach was exploding. He had never felt such a burning fire before.

When he reached the car, he fell up against it. He pushed himself upright and managed to get the door open. Then he fell in and stretched out on the seat. Something in his mind warned him that this wouldn't do at all. He sat up and managed to start the motor. As he slipped the car in gear he glanced at the people who had followed him out of the building. They stood around in a small group staring after him. He drove away slowly, fighting the steering wheel all the way.

The drive back across town was a nightmare for him. Whenever he stopped for a red light he almost passed out. The pain was something he had to cope with. "Sandra," he called the name, over and over again. Whenever he felt like quitting, he managed to call up an image of her.

When Chink stopped for a light at 87th Street, he felt as if the end had come. The front seat of the car was soaked with blood and his hands were coated with blood. He held his hand to his stomach, trying to push back the pain. If only his woman was there. The cars behind began to blow as the light had changed to green. He glanced up out of a fog of pain. He managed to push his foot down on the gas pedal and pull away from the light.

Sandra paced the floor back and forth. Ever since Chink had left, she had been up worrying about him.

Suppose he was hurt somewhere. He didn't have anyone he could turn to other than her. She made some
coffee but didn't have any taste for it, so she poured
it out. She started her pacing again, then glanced out
the window and noticed the nosy old caretaker water-
ing the lawn. He watched her staring out of the window, then raised his hand and waved. She didn't want
to acknowledge it, but she knew she'd better. He was
like an old woman, as she knew from the few times
she had spoken to him. He always had some kind of
gossip about the other people who lived in the building. The last thing she was interested in was what the
other people did. If they left her alone, she sure in
hell would leave them alone. He was just a nosy old
man, she reasoned, with nothing else to fill an empty
life other than an occasional glimpse into someone
else's affairs.

She turned away from the window in disgust.
Glancing out wouldn't bring Chink home. When he
finished what he had to do, he'd come home.

At 91st Street, Chink knew he was finished. He
couldn't go on. The fire inside him was too much. He
sat at the wheel, holding his stomach with one hand.
Sweat rolled off his brow. He could feel a tear rolling
down his cheek. "Now that's too much," he told himself. "Here I am crying like a bitch instead of gettin'
home to my woman." He caught the light and pulled
off again. One block, two blocks..., he counted them
off in his mind. He caught himself driving crazy with
the car going back and forth across the yellow line.

He talked to himself, cursing his own weakness. "I ain't nothin' but a poot-butt," he yelled out so that he could hear the sound of his voice. Again he called on his memory and a flash of his woman appeared before him. She was waiting with open arms. He was convinced he was going to die, and he knew then that he couldn't die without seeing his woman again. Just one more time, Lord, he prayed, then wondered about calling on the Lord. It was something he had never done before.

The lights began to play tricks on him. He couldn't tell the green lights from the red ones, and more than once he pulled out in front of oncoming traffic. Drivers slammed on their brakes and blew their horns angrily. He drove on, unaware of the confusion he left behind him. Finally he reached his neighborhood, yet he was unaware of that too. It was more like an animal instinct that made him turn on his street. He almost passed the apartment building but caught himself and pulled to the curb.

The old man in front of the building watched him closely. Chink didn't even see the old man. The pain was becoming so unbearable that he only had room in his mind for one thought: to see Sandra before he died. He was like a hurt animal, returning to his lair, searching for the place where he believed he could find peace.

He tried to open the car door, but he found that his strength had deserted him. To have come so far and yet not be able to finish the trip. He leaned over and one of his huge arms fell on the horn.

The sound was especially loud on the quiet street. The blare of the horn went on and on and Chink had passed out while lying on top of it.

The sound of the blaring horn brought Sandra on the run. She noticed the old caretaker moving toward the car. Damn, she cursed to herself as she reached the bottom of the steps. In seconds she was at the car door. She jerked it open and caught Chink's body as he fell out.

"Hold on, honey," she murmured, putting her arm around him. "Chink, you got to wake up," she yelled in his ear as she noticed the caretaker drawing near.

"Chink, Chink," she screamed at him. What to do, where to go, she thought to herself. If I go upstairs with him, the goddamn caretaker is sure to call the police!

"Move over, honey. Try and roll over," she said into his ear as she shoved at the heavy body. She knew at once that she couldn't go back up the steps. Before they could get up the steps the police would be at the door. So she got in beside him, pushing as hard as she could.

"Could you use some help?" The question came from the side of the car.

Sandra glanced up and saw the caretaker staring in. She knew at once that the man had noticed the blood all over the front seat of the car. "No, I don't need any help. I've got to get him to the hospital. He's been in an accident," she said as she started the car up. She tried to move him over another inch so that she could drive.

"You want me to go along with you to help you get him out?" the caretaker offered.

"No, thank you," she said flatly and pulled away from the curb. As she looked back in the mirror, she noticed him take a pencil out of his pocket and start to write.

"The bastard took the license number," she said, not really speaking to Chink but just speaking out loud.

"Sandra, Sandra, don't let them take me alive, baby. I told you I couldn't stand spending the rest of my life in prison," Chink managed to say as he struggled to sit up.

She glanced at him, thankful that he was still alive. "Don't worry, baby, I'll take care of you," she answered with more confidence than she felt.

Chink reached over and patted her leg, then he slumped down on the seat holding his stomach. "It burns so," he muttered over and over. "It's finished, honey. It's all over. We don't have to worry about our debt any more."

She smiled and patted him on the cheek. "I knew it was, Daddy, when I saw you in the car," she answered. "Chink, I don't know where to go unless I go back to our old apartment. I still got the key and the rent is still paid up." She glanced down at him to see if that was all right, but he was asleep.

She felt under his shirt for his heartbeat, and her hand came from under his shirt full of blood. "Don't

worry, Daddy, I'll take care of you," she murmured
as she turned a corner.

Sandra drove swiftly, cutting in and out of the traffic until she pulled up in front of their old apartment.
She parked as close as she could get, then bent down
and tried to wake Chink up. She knew it was impossible for her to get him up the steps without some
kind of help.

"Wake up, Daddy. I need your help. Just wake up
long enough to help me get you up the steps, then I'll
take care of that wound."

From somewhere in a deep fog Chink heard
Sandra's voice. He knew she was asking him to do
something. What was it? Wake up! The words came
over and over again. He fought to open his eyes.
Slowly he managed to sit up. A moan escaped from
him, but he did sit up.

"That's just great, Daddy," she said, then she got
out and went around the car. She opened the passenger door and grabbed one of his arms. She slowly
pulled him from the car. She put his arm around her
neck and started up the path. They made their way
slowly. The steps were a little more difficult, but they
managed to get up them. Sandra fumbled in her pocket and found the key. She opened the door and got
Chink inside, and he slipped to the floor as soon as
they entered.

12

DETECTIVES FISHER AND Horner walked out of Sammy's whisky store dumbfounded. He had been sure the man would help them, but it had turned out to be just the opposite. Sammy hadn't given them any information about Sandra. The main thing he had said was that, if she was in trouble, would the policemen please notify him so that he could come down and help the girl.

"Maybe we got the wrong girl," Horner said as they got in the car. "From what that old guy says, this girl would be an angel, not one who would allow herself to get mixed up in any kind of murder."

Fisher shook his head. "No, this is our girl all right.

She was arrested at school with Chink when he got busted for dope. She's no damn angel, you can bet on that. She's just a smart little bitch that's gotten in deeper than she probably wanted to."

Horner pulled away from the curb. "Well, Fish," he asked, "where to from here?"

"You checked with the probation department, Jerry. What was that address they gave you?" Fisher asked.

Horner motioned to some paper on the seat. "It's written down on that top piece of paper, but I don't think it will do any good. The probation worker said that, when she didn't report, he went by this address and the caretaker told him that he believed she had moved out. He'd seen her and another woman move some clothes out of the place."

Fisher was silent for a moment. "Let's go by and check out this guy's wife. Jimmy said she got a ride home with Sandra, so just maybe she was the broad that helped her to move." Fisher gave him the address and sat back and relaxed. He was beginning to like working with the quiet colored man. The young guy didn't ask too many silly questions. And above all, he didn't talk too much. If there was one thing Fisher hated, it was being stuck with an officer who talked all the damn time. He hated it.

In less than ten minutes Horner was parking in front of the address that Fisher had given him. The two men walked up the sidewalk together. Schoolchildren walking past gave the two officers plenty of room. They knew policemen when they saw them.

Shirley came to the door at once. She opened it wide. Both of the men noticed that she had been crying. "Won't you come in?" she said and stepped back, allowing the men room to pass.

"We'd like to ask a few questions," Fisher began as she followed them into the room. She motioned for them to sit on the couch.

"You'll have to pardon me," she said quickly. "I've just gotten the news about Jimmy. I don't know what could have gotten into him. He didn't have any reason to run," she stated flatly.

"We talked to him this morning," Horner said quietly, "and it seems as if this friend of his, Chink, talked him into running."

Shirley cursed angrily. "It must have been that way, because he sure didn't have any reason to run. I don't see how he allowed someone to talk him into running, though."

I don't either, Fisher thought coldly. The bastard probably ran on his own, or either begged the other kid to take him along. When he spoke it was altogether different from what he had been thinking.

"The only chance Jimmy has of clearing himself is for us to catch up with Chink. If we don't, Jimmy has this murder charge to ride out all by his lonesome." Fisher stated.

For a minute the men thought she was going to burst out crying, but she held back the flood of tears. "I don't know how I can help you," she said.

"Where do you think they might have gone?"

Horner asked quickly. "Any kind of information you can give us to where they might have gone to hole up. They have to have an apartment somewhere."

Shirley hesitated, then said quietly. "I don't know if it will help or not, but I went with Sandra to their old apartment where she picked up some clothes. Later on we went over on 110th. She didn't know that I knew about it, but she asked an old man who was working outside where the manager was, and he pointed out the manager's apartment." She glanced around to see if they were listening, then continued. "While she was inside the old man came over to the car and asked me if we were going to rent one of the apartments. I didn't know at the time if she was or not, but I figured she was. She stayed inside the manager's apartment about fifteen minutes and then came out. When she got back in the car, she tried to make me believe that she had stopped off to see a friend."

Fisher glanced over at his partner. "Can you remember what the address was?" he asked sharply.

"Yes," she answered, shaking her head. "It was simple to remember." And she gave them the address. "But I don't know what apartment she took. In fact I'm not even sure she took one, but I believe she did, I really do."

"So do we!" Fisher exclaimed quickly.

Both men got up at the same time. "We'll be checking with you," Fisher said as they started to go out.

Shirley followed them to the door. "I hope you will do what you can to help Jimmy out," she begged as the men prepared to leave.

"We'll do what we can," Fisher said over his shoulder, now in a hurry to get away from the woman with such misery in her eyes.

Fisher got in and drove. The men were silent on the short trip, each man deep in his own thoughts. Horner wished the end would come quick so that he could get home and get some sleep.

The call came over their radio about the killing of Tree. "Well, I'll be damn! I'll bet money it's got something to do with this case," Fisher stated as he speeded up.

"You think we ought to swing by there and check it out first, Fish, or go on over to the address we got?"

"Naw, the body will wait or be down at the morgue, but Chink won't. He might be preparing to leave town now. If we can catch him at this address we'll have the case busted wide open!" Fisher replied.

When they pulled up at the apartment building, there was a deputy sheriff's car already there. Since it was on 110th, it was out of the Los Angeles police department's jurisdiction. The two detectives got out and walked up the sidewalk. They met the single deputy coming down the walk.

Fisher stopped and showed his badge to the deputy. "What's going on here?" he inquired.

"I got a call to check out a man in a car who was supposed to be hurt," the deputy stated. "It seems as if some guy pulled up in a car but was too hurt to get out. He blew his car horn and this dame came running out of that apartment," he pointed over his shoulder, "and got in the car and pulled off."

The deputy pointed out the caretaker, who was standing in the background watching everything. "That old guy over there can fill you in. He's the one who made the call."

"Thanks," Fisher said and led his partner over towards the caretaker. The old man was only too glad to talk. He told them about all the blood he had seen in the car.

Horner walked back to the car and got the mug shot of Chink. He came back and stuck it under the old man's nose.

"Just a minute," the old man said and reached in his pocket and got out his glasses. He took one good look at the picture and said, "That's him, that's the boy I seen. I don't think I could ever forget that face, no sirree. I remember wondering to myself how such an ugly bastard ever got such a pretty woman. I mean, I don't know for sure if it's his girlfriend or not, but I ain't never seen her messin' with no other man. It seems as if this is the first man I've ever really seen her with. He was driving her car, I know that for a fact, 'cause I've seen her drive it too many times."

"Fine, that's just fine, old timer. You have really helped us out," Fisher said, making his getaway from the old man. He led the way back to the car and got in on the driver's side.

After he started the motor, Horner asked, "You don't think we should check out the apartment, Fisher?"

Fisher shrugged his shoulders. "I don't think it's really necessary this time, Jerry. We're more interested in putting our hands on this character Chink. I doubt seriously if there's anything we could find in the apartment that might put us onto them. If he's hurt, and hurt bad, from what the old man says, the girl is running scared. She has to find somewhere to take him. She didn't take him upstairs probably because of her fear of the caretaker calling the police." He hesitated briefly, then continued. "Just maybe, she might have gone back to her mother's house. She might believe they would be safe there, and besides, she could get some help. You got her mother's address there?"

Horner glanced through his papers. "Yeah, here it is." He quickly read off the address.

Fisher made a turn on Western and headed for the address. In minutes he was there. Horner jumped out and led the way up the filthy steps, stepping over trash that people had been too lazy to carry to the alley.

There was noise coming from the apartment. They stood outside the door listening. Fisher raised his fist and knocked. He had to knock again before there was an answer.

"Who the hell is it?" a woman asked in a husky voice.

"It's the police!" Fisher roared loudly. A sudden silence answered his reply. The door opened slightly.

"What do you want here? Ain't nobody called no damn police, and if they did, we ain't been making that much motherfuckin' noise!" the woman said belligerently as she opened the door the rest of the way.

"I want to ask you a few questions about your daughter," Fisher stated as he stepped into the room. Bottles were everywhere, with drunks sitting in the chairs and on the couch. He knew at once that the couple he searched for wouldn't be there.

"Well, I don't know anything about her or where she might be," the woman answered honestly. "I ain't seen her in over a month. She come by one day last month and left me a few dollars, but that's the last time I saw her, and that's the truth."

As the woman talked, Horner walked around the living room. He opened the bedroom and glanced in. Nothing. He gave up and came back to where Fisher was. The two men glanced at each other. There was an understanding that didn't need words. Both men realized that they were wasting their time.

Fisher removed a card from his pocket. "If you should see your daughter again, please get in touch with me. It will be for her best interests if you do," Fisher stated, realizing as he said it that the woman wouldn't pay any attention to him.

"I sure will," she replied, lying through her teeth. "Don't even worry about it. If she shows up around here why I'll just make her wait until I get in touch with you, officer."

"I know you will," Fisher said coldly as he started from the apartment. When they reached the hallway, he turned to Horner and spoke. "I can easily see why she left home at such an early age," he said quietly.

"Sometimes, when you see homes like that," Horner stated harshly, "you can't help but wonder why all the ghetto children don't turn out bad."

"That's crap, Jerry. You came up in the ghetto, but you're not mixed up in some shit like this." Fisher said coldly.

"I had parents that cared, Fish. They saw to it that I had everything they could give me. If it wasn't new clothes it was love and attention. Can you imagine that fuckin' bitch back there giving her daughter the love and care she needed. Shit," he continued, "these kids we're lookin' for, both of them should be going to school. Instead here they are out here in the streets, wanted for murder."

For one of the few times in his life Fisher was caught for words. He didn't know what to say. What Horner said was true, but pity was something they couldn't allow to come into their lives while working. Whatever the age of the suspect, murder had been committed, and they had a job to do.

13

SANDRA WASHED THE wounds carefully, and as she worked on them Chink slipped into the peacefulness of sleep. He tossed and turned but didn't wake up. She worked faster now, but there was only so much she could do. She realized that if she wanted Chink to live, she'd have to have a doctor for him. But where could she possibly get a doctor? And she couldn't stop the bleeding. Bleeding from the wound in his chest had stopped, but the stomach wound wouldn't. After she had him cleaned up, she sat on the floor beside Chink's prone figure.

He slowly opened his eyes. "Sandra, Sandra," he said, his voice sounding stronger as he talked. "I ain't goin' make it, baby," he stated.

She clutched his hand to her chest. "Don't say such things, Chink. You'll make it, honey, if I can get a doctor for you."

Chink shook his head. "That's death, baby. I don't want no doctor, honey. I mean that. If you get one, it will cause too much trouble. I got you in enough trouble already. If a doc comes, you'd have to hold a gun on him and make him take the bullets out, and I don't think he could do it here. Now listen, baby, I don't plan on going to no hospital, 'cause I don't want to end up spending the rest of my days in a prison. You hear, Sandra, I mean it, baby. I'd rather die than be locked up for the rest of my days, baby. I'm too young, honey, I couldn't adjust to prison life. I can't stand the bars. I damn near went crazy when I was locked up this time. The camp was all right, but not the county jail, honey. I mean it. I can't stand the bars!" He dropped back to the floor, holding his stomach.

"Chink, Chink," she cried, "you want me to get you on a bed, Daddy? Maybe it would be more comfortable," she said, crying all the time.

He managed to shake his head. "Baby, the floor is cool. I mean it. I slept on one all my life damn near, so it's only right that I die on one."

"You ain't goin' die, Daddy. You just ain't," she screamed.

He tried to smile at her. "It ain't nothing we can do about it, Sandra." He reached up and rubbed her cheek. "Baby, I wish you would leave. Ain't no way you can be really tied in with the killin', except that you picked me up on the highway, and there ain't no way for them to prove that unless you say something about it," he warned.

"Listen now, baby. When I'm gone, the police are going to give you a hard time, but if you do like I say, you can come from under it. It might be hard on you for a while but they'll have to cut you loose, baby."

"What about you, honey? What about you, Chink?" she asked crying.

"Don't worry about me. My life is finished, honey. I ain't goin' never leave this apartment alive. I can feel it, baby. I mean it. I'm above and beyond the reach of the police now, honey," he answered her slowly. As he held her hand he slipped back into the black recesses of unconsciousness.

As she stared down at his silent form, she wondered if she could slip out and go for a doctor. She knew where a black doctor was. If she took a pistol along, she believed she could force him to come along. She had almost made up her mind to go when he regained consciousness.

"For a minute I thought you had left me," he said as soon as he was awake. "Please don't leave me, Sandra; please don't go for no reason. Not until after I'm gone. Will you promise me that, honey? Please!"

She stared down into his face. The tears running down her cheeks fell on his upturned face. She dropped her head down on his chest, crying silently.

The sobs escaped from her slowly at first but then became louder.

He managed to raise his hand and stroke her hair. "Don't cry, baby. It ain't nothing to cry about. Think about all the good things we had together. Don't think about the worse, just the good. I'm just glad to be here with you, Sandra. Ain't nothing promised us, but we do have these few minutes together. Help me to cherish them, honey. Don't waste them crying."

She fought back the tears. I've got to be brave, she told herself over and over again. She raised her head and smiled down at him. "I understand, Daddy. I really do."

He grinned and tried to sit up. "Don't do that, Daddy," she cautioned as she saw the look of pain dash across his face. "Just relax. Don't strain yourself." She leaned down and kissed his cheek, then kissed him softly on the lips.

"Put something on the box, baby," he asked her quietly.

She glanced away, not wanting to remind him that the men had taken the record player when they robbed her. She got up and went over and put on the small radio that they had left behind. She found a good station playing the latest in soul music and left it there.

Chink didn't seem to notice the difference the radio made, or else he didn't mention it. Sandra glanced around for something to put under his head. Everything had been removed, as far as the pillows and bedding. She balled her sweater up and put it under his head. Slowly she washed away the bleeding, which seemed to be flowing faster. Again she had to fight back tears as she tried unsuccessfully to stop the flow of blood.

What can I do, what can I do, the thought ran through her mind. Now that he had made her promise not to leave, her hands were tied. There was no way she could go for a doctor now without breaking her word to him. If she left and he awoke and found her gone, he might just die while she was gone. If that happened, she would never be able to forgive herself. She would have missed his last moments alive, and she had come to accept the fact that he was going to die. There was nothing she could do about it except stay beside him and make his passing as easy as possible. One thing she promised herself, she would never let them take him alive. No, that she couldn't allow. For him to wake up in a prison ward was something she wouldn't allow to happen.

A thought flashed across her mind. "Chink, Chink, suppose I take you to a doctor's office and hold a gun on him until after he's closed your wounds. Then, Daddy, we might have a chance. We got the car. All we'd need is a running chance. With your wounds took care of right, you wouldn't have to think about dying."

"Hey, baby, let's be for real. There would be nurses to keep away from a phone. We'd need at least two good men with guns to hold off everybody." Chink reached up for her and she slipped down beside him.

"I can dig where you're coming from, but it just won't work. Why have my precious time wasted in a fruitless shootout, baby, when I can spend it so nicely with you?" He kissed her, a tender kiss that expressed all his love. Slowly he wiped the tears from her eyes.

"Honey," Sandra began, "I was only thinking about tomorrow. If we could get you together, Daddy, I believe we could make it." She felt in her heart that it was true.

She decided to try again. Nothing imagined could be too wild. "Honey, honey, I even believe that we could rip off a plane and go to Cuba or something, but don't give up on me. I'll go down with you, all the way, Daddy. I mean it. I don't care what we have to do, just tell me what and I'll go along with the program."

What could he say? How could you tell a woman that you love that the program is over. He'd never make it to the airport, and then she'd be alone. What good would he be if something started and he couldn't even stand up alone.

"Sandra, listen honey," he began. "There ain't never been no doubt in my mind about whether or not you would go along with the program. You been doing that ever since you became my woman. It ain't about that, baby. I wish it was some way I could make you understand. Nothing, nothing in this world could make me any happier than I am right now, holding you in my arms."

He started to cough and Sandra sat up. "Chink, can

I get you something? Maybe some water or something." She stared at him anxiously.

He managed to control the coughing. "Can you get me anything?" He rubbed her arm slowly. "Yes, if I could, there would be time enough for me to spend another night in your arms, if you could give me that, Sandra. If I make it up until tonight, let me sleep in your arms."

She grinned and got up. She reached down and tried to raise him. "It's night now, honey. Let me put you to bed."

He caught on to her meaning and struggled to rise. As the pain flooded through him, he thought about holding her again, in a lover's embrace.

Somehow she managed to get him on his feet. With all his weight across her shoulders, she dragged him to the bedroom. Slowly she undressed him, taking each piece off slowly, so that it wouldn't hurt him.

"Darling, you'd make a beggar's dream come true," he said tenderly from the bed. He lay back and drifted off into the foggish world of fever. He tossed and turned, moaning out. He imagined himself in the rear of the pool room where he had grown up. He was trying to sleep, but it was cold. The floor under him didn't seem to have any heat to it. He remembered slipping into the kitchen and trying to turn on the kitchen stove. Being too young to know how to light a fire, he had just turned on the knobs like he saw his father do. Then he had stretched out on the floor next to the stove. In what seemed like minutes, he remembered the light feeling that came to his head. He was about to slip off into sleep when he heard his father curse, then come running into the kitchen. The old man had slapped his face, then took him outside where he was made to walk and walk. He could still remember the biting cold that set in, once he was awake, and his father's drunken ignorance. His father walked him until early daylight, and he remembered that he prayed that he would never get that cold again.

Now he could feel the cold setting in. "Sandra, Sandra," he called out. Suddenly he felt something cold on his head and he tried to brush it away.

"Take it easy, Daddy, take it easy," she cautioned as she continued to wipe the sweat off his brow.

"Please, honey, please. The cold, I'm so cold. Take it away, please," he begged.

Quickly Sandra removed the face cloth, then she took off all of her clothes, except her panties and bra. She slipped under the cover next to him and wrapped her arms around his body. The flow of blood from his wound didn't disturb her, even though she could feel the warm blood on her stomach. She only gripped him tighter.

"Is that any better?" she asked, praying that her body brought him the warmth he sought.

"The cold, it's better, honey," he replied, holding her even closer.

They lay like that, giving comfort to each other, as the day began to slip away. From her he drew strength, and from him she drew faith.

14

HORNER WIPED THE back of his eyes with his hands. If they didn't quit soon, he'd fall to sleep in the goddamn car he believed. He glanced at his partner, who was sipping a cup of hot coffee. They had finally stopped for lunch. Horner folded up the cup and the napkin his hamburger had come in. Food wasn't what he'd wanted, but food was what he'd got.

"I got one more idea. I'd like to see out, Jerry, before we go in," Fisher stated as he finished with his food.

"What's that?" Horner asked, not too interested in what his partner had in mind. It had been too many hours without a stop, and now all he could see were red spots in front of his eyes.

"That apartment Jim's wife told us about. You know, the one she said Sandra picked up the clothes at. I'd like to check that one out before we call it a day," Fisher answered as he glanced up at his partner. He knew the young man was tired, but they were too close to ending it. He could feel it—the case was about to bust open.

Horner didn't feel like that at all. He believed the case could go on for days or weeks. It depended on how well the girl hid out. If she had found an apartment that they couldn't locate, it was good and possible. From all of her actions, she seemed to be smart.

As if he had read Horner's mind, Fisher spoke up. "The way I see it, she didn't have time to find another apartment. Either she's jammed up in a motel or she's gone back to one of her old places. There's nothing else she could do. With a wounded man, she hasn't too many chances."

"You're right about that," Horner agreed reluctantly, "but if she's in a motel, the only chance we have is someone picking up the license number on the car. You've got all the patrol cars checking out all the close motels, so it's just a matter of time. But if by chance she's got a friend with a house, we're in trouble; it might be a week or more before this case breaks."

"Yeah, I know all that," Fisher answered harshly, "but I just don't think it's going to go like that. No, they're young kids, and I don't think they know many people like that, plus the fact that he's wounded.

That's the big issue here. With him bleeding like hell, she has to be real damn careful where she takes him. You can bet on that part of it. As much as this girl cares about him, she's not going to take too many chances."

"I was thinking about what that guy's sister told us," Horner began. "If her brother hadn't stuck this girl up, I doubt if any of this crap would have happened. I guess that guy Chink must have blown his top when he saw his woman all beat to hell and back."

Fisher nodded his head as he started the motor and pulled out of the drive-in restaurant. "Yeah, I think from his actions he must have cared quite a bit for the girl. He killed everybody involved, as far as I can see."

As the men drove back across town, they talked the case over. They had just about put it completely together.

"The more I think about it, the surer I am that she doubled back to the apartment that she moved out of," Fisher said, nodding his head as he spoke.

And the more he talked about it, the more sure Horner became. He began to get the feeling that overcame him whenever he felt himself closing in on his prey. "It fits the picture all right," he stated.

Sandra finally got Chink to fall asleep peacefully. She waited until she was sure he was sound asleep before she got up. She slipped on her pants, then went into the kitchen to see if she could find something for them to eat. She prayed that she wouldn't have to go out to the store. She searched and found some cold lunch meat and a bottle of pop. It would have to do. She fixed two sandwiches, but common sense told her Chink wouldn't be able to eat his. How nice it would be if they were on the highway, maybe going to New York or someplace. She sat down and ate her sandwich while she daydreamed.

When she finished eating she got up and glanced out the window. Sandra froze in her tracks, as she watched the white man with his colored partner get out of their car. Cop was written all over them. As she watched them, they walked over to Sandra's car and opened the door. The two men talked amongst themselves for a few moments, unaware that the young girl upstairs in the window never took her eyes off them.

"Well, Jerry," Fisher said, "looks like we found what we came after."

"Yeah," Horner replied, "there's no doubt about it now. They're holed up here all right. You think we should call for help?"

"I don't think we'll need it, Jerry. The guy's been wounded, so the girl shouldn't give us too much trouble. She might be even glad to see us. That way she can get her man to the hospital."

Horner shrugged. He was thinking about the string of dead bodies that had led them down the couple's trail. "If you say so, Fish, but I'd feel a lot better off with a little more help," he said honestly.

"Okay then," Fisher replied, "if you feel that way

go on and call in. It won't take but a few minutes before we'll have more than enough reinforcements."

For a brief second, Horner felt ashamed. But then the vivid recollection of the last dead body came to him. He walked back to their car and called in. When he finished he joined his partner on the sidewalk.

Fisher wasn't going to wait for help. "Hell, man, if you feel too frightened, Jerry, I'll take care of it myself," he said as he went up the steps.

Before they had reached the stairway, Sandra had wheeled around and run into the bedroom. She glanced around wildly, looking for the pistols she had laid down. Snatching up one, she ran back to the window.

She waited until they were on the stairs, then broke the glass with the barrel. She quickly raised the gun and squeezed off a shot. The sound of the breaking glass had been all the warning the two detectives needed, though. Both men had jumped over the railing back down to the ground at the sound of the glass breaking. The shots had only given speed to their move.

Jerry Horner wiped the sweat from his brow. He glanced over at his partner. "Hey Fish," he called out with a smile, "I ain't seen you move that fast in I don't know how long."

Fisher had to smile back at his partner. Both men had moved so quickly that there hadn't been time for any kind of warning between them. "Yeah, it goes like that at times. I wonder who's handling that pistol up there," Fisher said, stroking his chin.

Horner only shook his head. "I don't know, but it seems as if they don't intend to give up easy."

"I'll tell you what I want you to do for me, Jerry," Fisher began. "I need a screen so that I can make it up those steps, so when I count to three, you pump a few shots into that window so that whoever is standing there will have to duck back. That will give me all the time I need to make it up the stairs."

Before the men could go into action, a patrol car pulled up. "Wait a minute, Fish," Horner called out. "Wait until them boys get over here, then we can both run up the stairs together."

The sound of three fast shots came to the waiting men. The patrolmen ducked back down behind their car. "You better yell out to them, so they'll know what to do. It looks like our help is pinned down," Fisher stated. "Slip around that way," he said, pointing out where a garage was built under the apartment building. "Go through there and give them their instructions, and I'll wait until you get back."

Upstairs, Sandra stared at the gun in her hands. She didn't want to accept the truth, that she was out of bullets. She tossed the gun down and walked into the kitchen. When she returned she went to the bed and sat down on it beside Chink. The noise of the shooting had awakened him and his eyes were bright as he stared at her.

"Hey, honey, the man done found us already, huh?" he asked, as he tried to hold her hand.

"Yeah, Daddy. They're outside," she answered, honestly, as she tried to hold back the tears.

"I only wish that it hadn't went like this, Sandra. There was so much we could have did together."

She only shook her head. What was there to say? In a few minutes the police would be inside the apartment. It was finished, all over.

Sandra picked up his hand and kissed it. "Honey, remember how peaceful it was the day we first walked home from school. The birds were singing, the sun was hot on our backs, and you were so bashful."

Chink smiled up at her. "I remember that and much more, honey. I remember every time we were together. It's something that nobody can take from us. You'll always have your memories, Sandra. Keep 'em and think about me sometimes."

The tears flowed down her cheeks unchecked. "How can I ever forget you, Chink?" She leaned over and kissed him. "You've given me the happiest times of my life, Daddy. I'll never be able to get you out of my mind. Never."

He smiled at her tenderly. "Remember your promise, honey. You ain't goin' let them take me out of here alive, baby. I don't want to die in no prison, 'cause if they get me to a hospital, they goin' do their damnedest to keep me living."

The sound of breaking glass came to them as the police shot out the front window. Under the hail of bullets, Fisher and Horner ran up the steps. Both men hugged the side of the building, breathing hard.

"Damn, I'm getting out of shape," Fisher said, breathing hard.

Horner glanced over at his partner and grinned. He knew how the older man felt, running up those steps. Expecting to be shot at was something he could do without. The men inched up to the door and then stood on each side of it.

Fisher raised his pistol and shot the lock off. Then Horner raised his foot and kicked the door in, and as soon as it flew open both men jumped into the apartment, each hitting the floor on a different side of the door. They glanced around the living room in astonishment, then Horner pointed out the empty gun on the floor.

Fisher crawled over to the gun and picked it up. He broke the gun open, then showed it to his partner so that Horner could see that the gun was empty. Both men glanced at the closed bedroom door.

Sandra knew that the policemen were in the living room. She glanced down at Chink. She could see the fear in his eyes as he stared up into her face. She leaned down and kissed him, and as she held him close he tried to put his arms around her, but it took too much of his strength. He dropped his arms back on the bed.

When Sandra finished kissing him, she raised up suddenly. The knife she kept concealed in her pants outfit flashed once in the afternoon sunlight as she brought it down quickly. She struck him in the chest, then pulled the knife out and struck again and he closed his eyes.

"You don't ever have to worry about them lockin' you up no more, Daddy," she said quietly and let the knife drop from her hand. She leaned over and began to sob, and when the bedroom door flew open she didn't even bother to glance up.

The two officers entered the room cautiously. They watched the couple on the bed warily. The sight was one that neither man would ever forget.

Sandra neither glanced up at the men nor acknowledged them. She continued to lie at the side of her man, crying deep sobs that seemed to come from the bottom of her soul.

From where they stood, they couldn't tell if she was hurt or not. Her arms and the white blouse she wore were saturated with blood.

"Don't worry, Daddy," they heard her say in a husky whisper. "You're free now, honey. They'll never lock you up again."

As they moved nearer the bed, Fisher noticed her hand fumbling around in the bedsheets. It was the only warning they had. She moved so fast that she almost caught them unaware. Her hand came up, clutching the knife she had used. Blood still dripped from the blade.

There was a blur of motion as she attempted to drive the dripping blade into her own frail chest. But Fisher moved fast. He grabbed her from behind, as his partner watched in surprise. There was a brief struggle before he could take the knife from her. Then all at once she crumpled up and fell on the side of the bed next to her lover. Though tears ran down her cheeks, there was no sound. Her grief was hers and hers alone. Whether she was tried for his death or not didn't make any difference to her now. All that mattered was that her man was free.

He was free at last.

Donald Goines
SPECIAL PREVIEW

KENYATTA'S ESCAPE

This excerpt from Kenyatta's Escape *will introduce you to one of Donald Goines' most popular characters—Detroit underworld kingpin, Kenyatta, whose exploits began with* Crime Partners *and* Death List *and conclude with* Kenyatta's Last Hit. *Ganglord Kenyatta has two ambitions: cleaning the ghetto of drug traffic and gunning down all the racist white cops. In* Kenyatta's Escape, *his war against both comes to a bloody, brutal confrontation in a suspenseful cross-country chase.*

THE POLICE LEFT Kenyatta's club on the north side of Detroit and headed toward Kenyatta's farm in the country. Some of the people there were making hurried efforts to leave. As soon as the club had been raided, Kenyatta had been called and duly informed. The few members inside the club hadn't stood up too long before giving out the information on Kenyatta's whereabouts. Kenyatta had expected just that. The members left at the club were occasional members and were not of the caliber of the hard-core members who made up the main part of the organization.

Kenyatta had every reason to be moving fast. For some time he had been actively working on two dream projects. First, he wanted to knock off every honkie cop who had it in for Blacks. And the attacks had been smoothly calculated and swift. Many a cop had never known what had ripped his guts open before the concrete came up to meet his face.

The second project was to rid the ghetto of all the junk pushers. The slick ones who drove the big hogs, who sometimes only fronted for the big men. Big men like Kingfisher, who sat up in a cool penthouse and raked in the money. Nickels and dimes turning into thousands of dollars. Black dollars!

And so Kenyatta had Kingfisher hit. And the word was out.

The four males who left the farm with Kenyatta were all armed to the teeth. Even the women who escorted the men were strapped down with deadly weapons. Jug and his girlfriend Almeta both carried a brace of .38 specials, while Eddie-Bee and his lady favored .44 magnums. Red and Arlene each carried sawed-off shotguns.

Kenyatta and Betty, with over thirty thousand dollars in a black briefcase, rode with Zeke and his Black queen. The couples piled into waiting cars in the farmyard and made haste to leave before the police arrived.

The rest of the people watched them go, not knowing when the leader would return to the farm. Ali, Kenyatta's brother, stood at the front door scratching his chin. He had been left in charge and that was almost all that mattered to him. The tall brown-skinned bald-headed man felt uneasy. But he couldn't

put his finger on it. There was no way for him to know
that his rule would last but a few hours.

Ali didn't have the knowledge that Kenyatta pos-
sessed. He was uninformed about the raid on the city
clubhouse, and he didn't know that an army of police
were on their way out to the gang's hide-out at the
farm at that moment. So he stood on the front porch
and swelled his chest, breathing the clean country air,
daydreaming about how sweet the future would be if
something happened to Kenyatta. He figures, he'd
have no problem stepping into Kenyatta's shoes and
taking over the smooth-running organization. Ali
looked over the farm buildings. The well-kept cabins
with their freshly painted doorways. Everywhere he
looked he saw young Black couples, dedicated men
and women who believed in their cause.

The drive to the airport was swift. Before Kenyatta
could finish smoking his second cigarette they were
turning into the lane that led to the terminal. When
they reached the busy terminal Kenyatta and his followers parked their cars in a no-standing zone. There
was no thought of returning to the automobiles. It was
time to get out. In the last short minutes at the farm
Kenyatta had briefed his small group again on their
plan of escape. It was well thought out and they had
been over and over it in practice runs in the past. Now
it was time to put it to use.

Everybody followed Kenyatta into the airport. As
he bypassed the ticket windows he turned and joked
with his followers. "Now that sure in the hell would

be a waste of good money, wouldn't it?" He shifted the heavy black bag containing the money around to his left hand.

All of the Black women carried large shoulder bags. Each couple had a certain amount of cash on them in case they ran into more trouble than they could handle and had to split. But none of them carried as much as Kenyatta did.

They waited about ten minutes until the regular passengers began boarding a nonstop flight to California. Kenyatta led his small dedicated group toward the loading ramp. The airport was set up in such a way that they didn't check for weapons until the passengers were going toward the ramp that led to the plane. Then you had to pass through a small space where they had a metal detector. Near the detector, a few guards stood around, looking bored, as they watched the metal detector to see if anyone was carrying a weapon.

When Kenyatta's group reached the guards, there was no suspicion. Kenyatta's group was well dressed and smiling. They came toward the detector slowly, acting as if they owned tickets, then suddenly all hell broke loose. Kenyatta pulled out an automatic. He waved it at the group of guards as his people came rushing up beside him. With a wave of his hand, Red went rushing up the ramp.

The sight of the Black men trying to commandeer the plane sent the guards into action. As Red came rushing past, one of the guards tried to reach out and

detain him with his outstretched arm while another
took a step back and pulled out his .38 police special
from his shoulder holster. Neither man found success.
The first guard took a bullet from Red's gun in the
face. Blood flew everywhere as the white guard crumpled in a heap on the floor. His face had been replaced
by a red gash. The young, attractive stewardess who
had been standing nearby screamed loudly as she
stared, horrified, at the dead man.

As the second guard came out with his gun Red's
woman Arlene, who was just a step behind her man,
shot from the hip and took the guard by surprise. His
first shot hit him high, the heavy slug smashing him
viciously in the chest and spinning him around. The
second shot took the back of the man's head off. The
couple ran past, not bothering to take a second look
as the object of their handiwork fell to the ground.

"Everybody stay still," Kenyatta ordered loudly,
"and won't nobody get hurt." As he spoke a guard on
Kenyatta's blind side made his move. As soon as the
man reached for his weapon, Betty stepped around her
man and raised the sawed-off shotgun she carried in
her bag. The gun was cut so short that it was almost
the same size as a pistol. She gave the guard both barrels. The shotgun kicked back in her hands so hard
she damn near dropped the weapon. Both barrels at
short range tore the man on the receiving end to
pieces. His stomach and chest dissolved before the
very eyes of the other watching men. Blood and guts
flew everywhere.

The sight of what the shotgun did froze the other guards in their tracks. Fear was written all over their faces. There was no doubt in their minds now as to whether or not the Blacks meant business.

Kenyatta backed up the ramp after taking the girl who had worked at the checkpoint as his shield. He stopped and waved Betty and the rest of his crowd past. They rushed up the ramp toward Red, who had the stewardess shaking from fear at the sight of his pistol.

Kenyatta's measured words roared out over the airport. "You honkies had better pay heed, or we'll kill everything white on the plane!" A dark flush stained his lean and shallow cheeks as rage glittered in his cold black eyes.

The sight of the terrified white girl in the tall Black man's arms made the guards hesitate. There was no doubt that he'd kill her. The guards held their weapons in check and allowed the wild-eyed Kenyatta to make his way on up the ramp.

Eddie-Bee stood at the top of the ramp waiting for him. He pointed two .38 short-nosed police specials at the white men standing at the bottom of the ramp.

"That's right," Kenyatta roared as he backed into the airplane, followed closely by Eddie-Bee. "If you don't want any dead passengers or stewardesses, keep your hands off them motherfuckin' guns!" His voice carried all the way through the plane, causing a near panic among the already frightened passengers.

The members of his gang had already taken complete command of the airplane. The pilot was well aware of the fact that his plane had been commandeered by a bunch of Black gunmen. He reached the tower by radio and asked for information on what to do.

"Follow their orders. Don't endanger any of the passengers' lives," the voice from the tower replied. "The people who have taken control of your plane are murderers. They have just killed at least four people that we know of in the terminal. For Christ's sake, be careful!"

The co-pilot glanced over at his captain and their eyes locked for a quiet moment. But that was broken by Zeke's sudden entrance. The tall Black man stood in the cockpit with a cocked gun in his hand.

He aimed it at the back of the co-pilot's head. "It won't be any trouble if you don't give us any," the Black man stated harshly.

From the way the man had spoken, the pilots knew he meant business. "Where to?" the captain inquired softly.

"When we get off the ground I'll personally let you know," Zeke replied, then smiled. It had gone easier than Kenyatta had said it would. "Wherever we go," Zeke said offhandedly, "you can bet it will be where a Black man is treated like a man. Yes indeed!" Zeke was speaking more to himself than to the white pilots. "It's goin' sure 'nuff be where a Black man can be a man!"

2

KENYATTA STOOD AT the open hatch of the airplane until the men removed the ramp. The airplane was ready now to take off. As the door closed he walked slowly up the aisle, his sharp glance taking in the way his members had everything under control. All of the passengers were sitting quietly in their seats, watching the proceedings out of fear-ridden eyes. Most of them were looking for the sudden arrival of the police, but as the jet engines started up, this hope died quickly. The sound of the jets roaring shattered the hopes of just about all the passengers. Now, they had only to look forward to a deadly ride to God knew where. Each passenger huddled in his seat, wondering wildly where it would all end. As Kenyatta walked past, most of them glanced down at the floor, afraid to look him directly in the eye.

Sitting in the rear of the airplane, private guard James Carson tried to catch the eye of Will Coney, a flight marshal hired by the airlines. When Carson finally managed to catch Coney's attention, the marshal held up a finger for patience. Carson settled back in his seat and began to put his seatbelt on. The pilot's voice came over the speaker informing all the passengers to do the same.

As soon as Kenyatta heard the pilot's voice, he walked to the back of the plane and motioned to the fat white man sitting in the last seat by himself. "Okay, honkie," Kenyatta ordered sharply, "you better get up front and find you another seat." Kenyatta stared at the white man closely. For a second he didn't believe the white was going to do as he said. He had just about decided to blow the man's brains out when the fat man got up slowly from his seat and started up the aisle.

Kenyatta stared after the middle-aged white man. He could read the dislike in the man's eyes, but there was something else there that he hadn't been able to read. At that moment he decided to take a closer look at the honkie later on. For the moment, though, Kenyatta settled down in the seat. Betty came rushing from the front of the airplane and joined him, just as the pilot warned everybody again to fasten their seatbelts.

Private guard James Carson settled down in the seat beside Detective Will Coney. "Goddamn it," Will cursed under his breath, "why didn't you pick another seat somewhere. We don't want these jigs to get suspicious of us."

"It's all right," James assured him. "That tall nigger made me move out of my rear seat, so he don't suspect nothing."

Will let out a sigh. "I hope the hell you know what you're talkin' about, Carson, because these niggers are playing for keeps."

"I believe we can take them, Will," Carson stated, his voice revealing more than anything else his urge for action.

"Take hell," Will replied. "Are you out of your fuckin' skull? Listen, Carson, don't start no hero shit on this trip, because we're outnumbered and don't stand a chance in hell of takin' all these jigs by surprise! So don't get no fuckin' ideas that might get some innocent passengers killed. No sir," Will continued, "we're just along for the ride on this one, unless something comes up that we can't overlook. Then maybe we'll have to toss off our cover. But not until!"

The words that Will Coney spoke went in one ear and out another. James Carson had no intention of letting such a good opportunity get past him. If he could somehow regain control of the airplane for the airline, his picture would be in every paper in the country. It was too good a chance for him to pass up. He might go a lifetime and never get another opportunity like this one. That he might lose his own life in the endeavor never entered his mind.

"Will," Carson answered, "if they start knockin' off the passengers, I don't plan on sitting on my fat ass and just watching them, I can tell you that much!"

"Yeah, Carson, let's worry about that one when we are confronted with it. So far, they haven't bothered anybody on this flight yet."

"What the hell you think all that goddamn shooting was about just a few minutes ago?" Carson demanded sharply.

"Whatever it was, it didn't concern us. Our job is to take care of the people on this airplane, Carson. Whatever went on at the terminal was up to the guards that worked there." Before Carson could say anything, Will continued. "They came aboard so fuckin' quick I didn't know what the hell was happenin' until I was staring down the barrel of a double-barreled shotgun that one of them fuckin' cunts was handling."

James Carson let out a curse and stared down angrily at the smaller man next to him. "I wish to hell I would have got a break like that with only some fuckin' broad covering me. I don't think them fuckin' women really know which end is up. Shit, Will, you should have took the fuckin' thing from her and rammed it up her fuckin' cunt!"

Will laughed good-naturedly. "I didn't see you taking any weapons from anybody, Carson."

"Hell, I didn't have any woman covering me either.

That little light-skinned bastard had two fuckin' pistols aimed at me before I knew what was happening!" Carson stated sharply, as he remembered the embarrassing incident.

"Well, don't worry about it," Will warned. "Maybe it's best we didn't show our hand, because there's at least eight of them that I'm sure of. Two of us can't do very much against that many odds. And you keep that in, buddy."

Carson glared at the other man but didn't make any comment. His mind was wandering. He pictured himself getting off the airplane as newspapermen fell over each other trying to reach him for an interview. The more he dreamed about it, the wilder his imagination became. He could see himself explaining it over and over again to beautiful women. Blondes, redheads. His mind held vivid pictures of movie stars..., all of them were now at his feet. He could see himself being cold and aloof as he told of the gun battle that he had won as he took back control of the airplane. The thought was so pleasant that for the next hour Carson sat back in his seat and just dreamed.

Kenyatta sat quietly next to Betty and spoke in glowing tones of the new world they would find when they reached their destination, Algiers. The trip so far had been so peaceful that most of the Black men and women had relaxed, quite sure that they now had the airplane well under control.

Breaking off his conversation, Kenyatta waved his hand in the air so that he could catch the attention of one of the stewardesses who were standing in the rear of the plane. As the woman approached, Kenyatta spoke to her quietly. "Why don't you and the other girls begin serving the passengers their dinners."

The woman stared at him with frightened eyes, but the softness of his voice slowly removed most of the fear. She attempted to smile as she nodded her head in agreement. She went back and spoke to the other woman. Soon every passenger who could eat had a tray of food.

As the time slowly went past, Kenyatta glanced out the window and noticed that it was still light outside. He glanced at his watch and was surprised to see that it was past eight o'clock in the evening. An hour later he glanced at his watch again and frowned after seeing that it was still daylight.

With his temper slowly rising, he made his way up toward the front of the plane. As he walked past his friend Jug, Jug spoke up. "Anything up, Brother?"

Kenyatta shrugged his shoulders. "I ain't hip, Jug, but I think the pilot is trying to play games with us."

Even though he hadn't spoken loud, his heavy voice carried through most of the airplane. Before Kenyatta had finished speaking, he was joined by Red and the smaller built Eddie-Bee.

Kenyatta smiled as the two men came up. "Hold on, brothers, it don't take all this. I just want to check out something, that's all." He waited until the two men returned to their seats before continuing on his way.

Without hesitation Kenyatta pushed his way into

the cockpit. The pilots glanced up in surprise when
he entered. "Maybe I made a mistake, boys," Kenyatta
began, "by not introducing myself earlier. I happen to
be the big bad nigger who's running this fuckin' thing,
and I think somebody is trying to put shit in my game.
Do you guys dig where I'm coming from?"

The two pilots glanced at each other, not understanding what the tall Black man meant. "I'm afraid
we don't," the captain answered honestly.

"Why don't we try it again, then," Kenyatta said.
"First of all, the time situation is fucked up and when
I say fucked up, I mean just that. Now, by my motherfuckin' watch, it's nine-thirty in the evening. And
any goddamn country boy can tell you that at that time
of the evening it should be more than dusk outside."
Kenyatta pointed out the window. "But when I look
out like now, for instance, it ain't even that. So I got
to wonderin' just what the fuck is going on. I know
you been told that our destination is Algiers, so why
the fuck is this time element shit coming up?"

The two pilots glanced at each other nervously
before the captain replied. They had discussed the
matter between themselves earlier so they came out
with their prepared lie immediately. "We are nearing
the West Coast. We will have to land to take on fuel
in California. So the reason you still see daylight is
because of the difference. You will have to set your
watch back three hours if you want it to be correct
now."

As the captain spoke, Kenyatta stared into the white

man's eyes trying to tell if he was lying. He didn't know if they should land in California or Cuba to take on fuel. It was something he should have been aware of, but he wasn't. He could only hope that the pilot spoke the truth.

"Listen buddy," Kenyatta said, still keeping his voice low, "I'm not going to warn you again because we are not playing games. If I find out you're fuckin' around, I'm going to blow your shit out, you understand?"

He stared first at the pilot, then he glared at the co-pilot, so that neither man really knew who the warning was for. Though neither man knew for sure, they each felt that the Black man meant every word he said. There was something about the tall man that made them respect his words. They watched as he turned his back on them and left the cockpit.

When the co-pilot reached for the radio, the captain brushed his hand away. "No," he warned, "we have followed orders and have flown toward California so that they will be ready when we land in Los Angeles. There's no reason for us to take any more chances than we have al...."

That was as far as the captain got. The door opened quietly and Kenyatta stood in the doorway. As the two white men glanced around, the first thing they noticed was that this time he wasn't empty-handed.

The pistol seemed to grow larger and larger as the two men stared into the short barrel of the snub-nosed .38. The clean-headed Black man seemed to be smiling as he raised the gun. At the last minute, the co-pilot realized that the gun was pointed in his direction. He started to rise from his seat when the first gunshot exploded in the tiny compartment. The concussion from the gun almost broke their eardrums.

The bullet caught the co-pilot in the side of his forehead and came out of the other side of his head. Brains and blood splattered the windshield. As his co-pilot fell against the paneling the captain stared in shocked horror. He couldn't believe what he saw. The fact that his friend had been killed in cold blood was too much for him to accept. His eyes bugged outward and for a minute his face paled so much that it seemed as if he was having a stroke.

Without hesitating, Kenyatta raised the gun and aimed it at the captain. "If I have to, man, you'll be next." From the look in his eyes the captain believed every word the Black man had spoken.

Before the captain could get himself completely under control, all hell broke loose in the rear of the airplane. The two men in the cockpit could only stare behind them, dumbfounded.

The sounds of gunfire coming from the cockpit set the stage for violence. At the first gunshot most of the Black men rushed toward the front of the plane. As they gathered in front of the thin doorway, undecided on whether or not to break in, they appeared to be very vulnerable.

At the sight of the men standing there confused, Carson saw an answer to his dreams. Here was the

wonderful opportunity that he had prayed for. There
was no doubt in his mind whether or not they could
take the confused men. The women didn't disturb him
whatsoever, because he was sure that they would just
toss their guns down once things began to get hot. He
didn't even bother to consult Will Coney.

Reaching under his arm, Carson drew out his pistol and opened fire. At the first sight of the gun in
Carson's hand, Will cursed under his breath. He did-
n't bother to argue because it was too late. Carson was
committing them to a lopsided gunfight that couldn't
have but one ending.

Will was a man who faced life without any false
beliefs. What was white was white, what was black
was black. It was as clear as that. Now, as he pulled
out his gun, he knew that death was the only thing
that they would get out of the gunfight. The odds were
too long, it was impossible for them to win.

The passengers inside the plane began to scream.
Most of them were white. Three Black women traveled with a Black man and, at the sight of the guns
in the white men's hands, the Black man tried des-
perately to get the three women to lie down out of the
way.

The first shot from Carson's gun took the tall dark-
complexioned Zeke in the back. He had been standing at the rear of the crowd of Black men, waiting to
find out what was happening inside the cockpit. The
impact of the bullet knocked him into two of the other
men.

Before they could react to the sudden ambush, another shot rang out and this time the short husky Red was hit. He spun around from the shock of the slug, but managed to stay on his feet. The bullet had struck him high in the left shoulder. As Carson drew down on the bewildered bunch of men again, the Black women went into action.

Zeke's woman Ann let out a scream of rage as she saw her man go down. It took a moment for her to find out where the gunshot came from. In her rage and hurt she had first started to run up the aisle toward the stricken man. Then, at the sight of the two white men with guns in their hands, she tried to pull up. Her sawed-off shotgun was just coming up when Will took careful aim and shot her in the chest. The force of the bullet knocked the tall brown-skinned woman off her feet and on top of a white woman passenger.

Betty, using the same cold, deadly concentration that her man Kenyatta used, fired slowly from the hip with the short .44 magnum she carried. The bullet took Will an inch over the heart, killing him instantly.

The sounds of the gunshots and screams of the frightened passengers caused bedlam on the large airplane. One woman passenger jumped up from her seat, screaming in panic, and began to run wildly up the aisle. The Black men at the front of the plane now stood with their backs to the cockpit as they searched frantically for their ambusher. The sight of the screaming woman was too much for one of them. Eddie-Bee couldn't control his reflexes. After throwing down the fleeing woman, his trigger finger finished what he hadn't meant to do. He squeezed off a shot, taking the woman in the back. She staggered from the blow, then continued to run until one of the Black women raised a gun and put her out of her misery. The bullet took the woman in the forehead.

Carson was still on his feet. Somehow he had managed to escape being hit. As he raised his gun again, it dawned on him that he was fighting a losing battle. The sight of his dead companion beside him brought home the truth of the matter. Now there were no more daydreams. What Will had tried to warn him about was coming true. There would be no large parades with him as the main event. The hero of the moment was only dreaming. The only thing he would get out of this was a hero's death. No beautiful women would be flocking around begging to be in his company. Now there was only the chance of taking some of his killers with him. After taking a quick glance over his shoulder, the blood froze in his veins. The Black women he had so readily ignored were all armed, and before he could take his eyes off them, he saw at least three of them pointing weapons at him. The barrage that struck him was awesome. He was dead before ever reaching the floor.

After Carson's death, the sounds of gunfire died out. People stared around at the carnage—bodies were everywhere.

Betty leaned down and felt Ann's pulse. When she rose there were tears in her eyes. "The sonofabitch killed her," she cursed.

Red's short brown-skinned woman, Arlene, started up the aisle toward her man, who was stretched out on the floor. As she passed the three Black passengers, one of the women started to scream at her.

"What's wrong with you folks? You ain't nothing but animals, that's all! Just goddamn animals! You all need to be dead somewhere," the woman cursed. "Just killin' people like you ain't got good sense. Makes me shame to be Black."

All at once Arlene lost her reasoning. The sight of her man lying on the floor and now this woman screaming in her face was too much. Without hesitation, Arlene raised the pistol she carried and fired pointblank at the Black woman in front of her. The force of the bullet took the woman in the breast and lifted her off her feet. She fell back amongst her friends, dead.

Arlene waved the pistol at the rest of the group of Blacks. "Now, has any more of you self-righteous motherfuckers got anything else to say?" Her eyes went from one face to the other. Each one clamped their mouth shut, knowing their life depended on silence.

As she went on past the group, Betty walked up and warned them. "Your friend brought that on herself. I hope the rest of you learned something from it. We wouldn't have hurt none of you. All you had to do was remain silent and stay the fuck out of the way. Now, one of your comrades is dead, just because she couldn't keep a lid on her mouth. Let's hope that the rest of you value your lives more than she did, because this is no game we are playing. This is for keeps, so just keep it in mind." Betty walked on toward the front of the plane. Suddenly the airplane went into a nose-dive, throwing Betty off her feet. Everyone was jolted out of place as the airplane went out of control.

The sudden nosedive took Kenyatta by surprise, too. He was tossed on top of the control panels. As he fought to regain his feet, he noticed the captain bent over his controls. The man was fighting to regain the control of the airplane, but Kenyatta could tell from his actions that he was hurt. There was blood all over the back of his chair.

"Pull it out, captain," Kenyatta ordered sharply, as he struggled to get into the co-pilot's seat.

Just when it seemed as if they would never come up out of the dive, the pilot finally managed to regain some control of the plane. The plane straightened out, but the pilot was slumped over the controls.

SPECIAL PREVIEW SECTION FEATURE

Ganglord Kenyatta has two ambitions: cleaning the ghetto of drug traffic and gunning down all the racist white cops! But a black and white detective team has been on his tail.

INCLUDES SPECIAL PREVIEW SECTION

#1 AMERICA'S BEST SELLING BLACK AUTHOR

Donald Goines

THE TORRID ADVENTURE THAT TORCHES A
PITCHED BATTLE BETWEEN KENYATTA AND
"THE MAN"

KENYATTA'S ESCAPE

They discover his army's camp and, armed with tanks, bring a bloody Doomsday to his followers. But Kenyatta hijacks a jet liner, ready to shoot his way into the biggest Black crime wave ever!

In *Kenyatta's Escape* author Donald Goines continues his story of the bloody, brutal world of crime started in *Crime Partners* and *Death List*. They're all back, for a coast-to-coast chase that will spell gripping adventure!